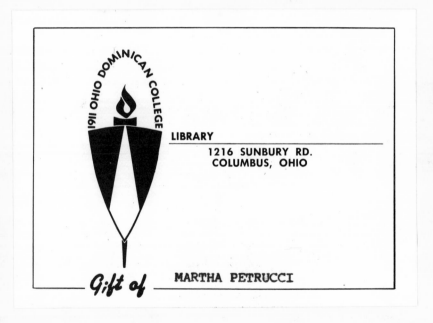

The Ghost of the Gravestone Hearth

Also By Betsy Haynes

Cowslip
Spies on the Devil's Belt
The Against Taffy Sinclair Club

BETSY HAYNES

The Ghost of the Gravestone Hearth

publishers since 1798

THOMAS NELSON INC., PUBLISHERS

Nashville   New York

Copyright © 1977 by Betsy Haynes

All rights reserved under International and Pan-American Conventions. Published in Nashville, Tennessee, by Thomas Nelson Inc., Publishers, and simultaneously in Don Mills, Ontario, by Thomas Nelson & Sons (Canada) Limited. Manufactured in the United States of America.

First edition

Library of Congress Cataloging in Publication Data
Haynes, Betsy.
    The ghost of the gravestone hearth.
    SUMMARY: Charlie's summer at the beach promises to be uneventful until the ghost of a sailor who died in 1712 persuades him to help dig for buried treasure.
    [1. Buried treasure—Fiction. 2 .Pirates—Fiction 3. Ghost stores] I. Title.
PZ7.H314913Gh   [Fic]   77-1978
ISBN 0-8407-6544-4

FOR MY MOTHER

who likes ghosts almost as much
as baseball

CHAPTER 1

CHARLIE POTTER slipped his army-surplus gas mask on and headed for the beach. Maybe a bomb filled with deadly nerve gas would wash ashore from some sunken World War II aircraft carrier, and he would have to disarm it singlehandedly before it exploded and killed everyone along the Connecticut shore of Long Island Sound. Well, at least it was better than sitting around in his crummy room listening to his crummy clock tick.

Charlie wished that his parents hadn't rented that crummy old beach house for the summer, anyway, especially since his father only came down on weekends, and he was stuck the rest of the time with his mother and his sister, Nanabelle, who was going to be a freshman in college this fall and was the world's most boring person. There was nothing to do and no one to play with. It was just plain crummy.

They had only been there one week, but already he missed his house in Poughkeepsie and playing baseball with his buddies so badly that he almost couldn't stand it. But most of all he missed his best friend, Henry Ward. Charlie and Henry had lots of plans. Their favorite thing in the world to do was to sit in

Charlie's tree house and talk about how when they got older they were going to buy a motorized camper and drive around, getting jobs wherever they pleased so that they could see all of North America, Central America, and South America. After that, they would put their camper on a ship and head for Africa.

Charlie tried not to think about Henry and the motorized camper. It only made him sad. Instead, he concentrated on scanning the beach for anything resembling a bomb.

There was a strip of private beach that went with the house the Potters had rented, and Charlie marched up and down for a while poking at broken shells, sea lettuce, and beer cans and an occasional piece of driftwood. Finally he stopped with a sigh. There wasn't a single solitary bomb to be found. He sat down in the warm sand and looked out across the water. There was nothing out there, either, except for a couple of sailboats and a fleet of sea gulls that rode the swells not far from shore. He tried to pretend that the sea gulls were U-boats and that he was hiding in a bunker on shore ready to pick them off when they got close enough, but his heart wasn't in it.

Charlie looked up and down the long row of beach houses hoping to catch sight of someone near his own age. The houses were set close together, and all had porches and lots of big windows looking out toward the water. Each one, like Charlie's, had a narrow strip of private beach. Mostly the private beaches were deserted, although a few people lounged around here and there, but not a single one of them appeared to be a prospective playmate. Looking past the row of

summerhouses, Charlie eyed the public beach longingly. Kids were running and splashing, the lifeguards
were blowing their whistles, and people were sunbathing and eating picnic lunches. He wished that his
parents would led him go to the public beach. He
could probably find someone to play with there. But
it was no use. His mother always screwed up her face
when he asked to go and started raving about how
crowded it was and how people always kicked sand in
your face and how Charlie might swallow some water
that some little kid had peed in and get sick or something. Then she would start in about how lucky they
were to have such a beautiful beach all to themselves
and how so many kids lived in ghettos and stuff and
never got to spend the summer at a beach at all.

The sun was beating down on his gas mask, and
it was stuffy inside. Rivers of perspiration rolled down
Charlie's face and into his eyes, so he pulled off the
mask and pitched it into the sand. He sat there looking at it, feeling a lump growing in his throat, and he
thought about Henry again and about all the fun that
he could be having back in Poughkeepsie.

As he sat there, he began to have the creepy feeling that someone was watching him. Charlie looked
quickly around, but no one was nearby. The feeling
wouldn't go away, and he shivered nervously in the
warm sun and looked around again, this time more
slowly. On the sand about four houses away a girl in
a red bikini was sunbathing. Charlie knew that it
couldn't have been her he'd felt looking at him because she was lying on her stomach with her feet
toward him. Besides, she looked as if she were asleep.

Farther down the beach, a man tossed a ball for a big black dog to chase, and a lady helped a baby put sand in a pail, but they weren't paying any attention to Charlie, either.

Then he scanned the top of the seawall that separated the beach from the yards, just in case some little kid was crouched there playing I spy or hide and seek, but there was no one there, either. Even the sailboats that had been on the Sound just a moment before had glided swiftly out of view. There was no doubt about it, he was alone except for a sprinkling of sea gulls that dotted the beach.

Charlie tried to think about something else. If he could get his mind off of the eerie feeling that he had, maybe it would go away. He tried to concentrate on some adventure that he and Henry would have in their motorized camper. Maybe they would be crossing the desert and come upon a coven of witches making bloody sacrifices. And maybe the witches would take out after them and try to put a spell on them. Charlie shivered even harder. He was only making himself feel worse.

Just then a sea gull that had been circling overhead swooped down and landed on Charlie's gas mask. At first he didn't pay much attention to the gull. The shore was always crowded with them, some half tame from scavenging on public beaches. Besides, it looked like all the other sea gulls. It had the same white breast and gray wings tipped in white, and its beak curved downward and it stood on sturdy-looking gray legs. Still, there was something about it that made Charlie feel uneasy.

All of a sudden he realized that the sea gull was staring straight at him with black, beady eyes. Surely it wasn't just a sea gull's eyes that he had felt upon him a moment before. Why would a sea gull stare at anybody, anyway? he wondered. But this sea gull *was* staring, and it was staring at Charlie.

Charlie's heart began to pound, and his scalp had a tickly feeling, as if forty spiders were dancing in his hair. He looked away. There were at least a dozen other sea gulls on the beach. They were mostly strutting around and pecking in the sand, and not one of them was giving him so much as a second glance. What was the matter with this one? Was it sick or something?

He looked at the gull again. Its shiny black eyes were still glued to him. Charlie thought about the witches in the desert and their spell. Maybe this sea gull was part of some evil spell. Maybe he should get out of there while he still had a chance.

Charlie jumped to his feet, and the sea gull flew screaming into the sky. It seemed to hesitate in midair right above Charlie's head, screaming louder than ever before it flew away. Without looking back, Charlie grabbed his gas mask and hightailed it for the house. He went straight to his room and closed the door. Then he hurried to the window and looked down at the beach. Sea gulls were everywhere. Some of them hunted for food in the sand and others rode the air currents like graceful white kites. They all looked perfectly harmless.

Charlie stayed by the window for a long time, watching for signs of strange sea-gull behavior, until finally he began to feel a little foolish. He knew that Henry would probably laugh his head off if he ever found out that Charlie had been spooked by a sea gull. He decided to forget about the whole thing, and by bedtime he was feeling perfectly normal again. In fact, Charlie might have forgotten all about staring sea gulls and evil spells forever if he had not had a very strange dream that night.

As he slept, the dream appeared, entering his mind with the slow gentleness of a dim photograph floating to the surface of a pool. It seemed to be nothing more than a small fire, far away, at the end of a long, black tunnel. It crackled and spat merrily, but, oddly enough, it cast no light whatsoever on its surroundings.

The fire seemed to be moving slowly toward Charlie, and as it moved he could feel its heat increasing so that a cozy warmth spread over him. The dream hovered in his sleeping mind for a moment and then slipped away as softly as it had come, taking its warmth with it.

At that instant a sea gull screamed, and Charlie awoke with a start. He was shivering, but he pushed himself upright and hugged his pillow while he peered around the silent bedroom. A peculiar light filled the room, the same sort of gray glow that comes just before dawn, but outside his window the night was a starless black. Where was the strange light coming from? thought Charlie, his blood pounding in his temples. And why had the fire in his dream shed no light at all? And where was the sea gull that he had heard scream just now? Was it the same one that had stared at him on the beach?

Gradually the light faded, just the way the fire in his dream had faded and disappeared. Only the clock on the nightstand shone luminously. It was ten minutes after three.

Charlie told himself as sternly as he could that it was just his imagination, and he slid down under his covers so that only his nose stuck out. It was morning before he went back to sleep.

CHAPTER 2

WHEN CHARLIE awoke the next morning he could hear the old water pipes jolting and groaning downstairs in the kitchen. His mother was putting on the coffee.

The pipes never jolted and groaned in their house back in Poughkeepsie. It was a great house. But then, everything jolted and groaned in this old place. His mother had told him that it had been built around the turn of the century and that it had been remodeled a jillion times by a bunch of different owners. That was probably why some of the walls didn't meet quite right and the whole place seemed sort of flimsy.

Nanabelle loved this house. Nanabelle would, he thought. There was a long porch that ran the entire length on the side overlooking the Sound, and at night Nanabelle would put on her long robe and stroll up and down the porch and gaze at the moon. His mother always said that Nanabelle was a romantic, but he thought that she was definitely cracked. Why couldn't she be like Henry's older sister, Polly. She wanted to be a doctor and was always doing neat things like dissecting dead frogs.

By the time Charlie was dressed, the smell of

14

bacon had floated up the stairs and into his room, and his stomach grumbled expectantly. His sleepless night had left his eyes feeling as if they were filled with gravel, but in the daylight his strange dream did not seem half as scary as it had appeared in the dark.

Charlie was whistling a tune as he hurried down the stairs and into the kitchen. He stopped short at the door. Nanabelle was sitting at the breakfast table sipping a cup of coffee and looking about as jolly as Dracula's mother. There was only one thing that would get Nanabelle out of bed before noon. New clothes. So he wasn't surprised when his mother looked up and said, "Good morning, Charlie. Nanabelle and I are going into Bridgeport to look for some school clothes for her. Would you like to come along?"

"Oh, great!" said Nanabelle, looking as if she would throw up. Charlie was going to say that he would love to go, just to see if she really would, but he changed his mind because the idea of following the two of them in and out of ladies' dress shops for an entire day made his stomach feel a little floppy, too.

"No, thanks," he said. "I think I'll stay home and work on my shell collection."

His mother nodded absentmindedly and slid a fried egg onto his plate. Charlie was sorry that he had mentioned the shell collection since he didn't really have one, and he was a little hurt because his mother was so busy getting Nanabelle ready for college that she didn't even know that.

"That's fine, dear," she said. "But don't wander off somewhere because according to the paper it's supposed to storm this afternoon."

Charlie pretended to be absorbed in chasing a piece of bacon around the rim of his plate with his fork and didn't answer. A super plan was forming in his mind, and if he promised to stay home for the day, he would have to abandon it.

As soon as he had finished breakfast, Charlie slipped back up to his room. He was a spy preparing for a secret mission, and he closed the door and listened for a moment to make sure that no one had followed him up the stairs. As soon as he was satisfied, he slipped off his jeans and put on his swimming trunks. Then, pulling his jeans back on, he was disguised as an ordinary boy again. No one would ever suspect that he was about to infiltrate the public beach.

After that there was nothing to do but wait, and it seemed like hours before his sister and mother were ready to leave the house. He understood about his mother. She always redesigned her entire face. But what made Nanabelle so slow was a total mystery, since she didn't wear any makeup, and her hair just hung down her back as limp as string.

Finally the car pulled out of the driveway, and Charlie went into action. He grabbed a towel out of the bathroom and raced to the kitchen, where he made himself a peanut-butter-and-jelly sandwich to take along for lunch. On the way out the door, he stopped. This mission was going to be dangerous, so he went back to the kitchen for a cyanide pill, which looked just like a chewable vitamin. Slipping the cyanide pill into the sack with his sandwich, Charlie knew that he was as ready as he would ever be, so he left the house and hurried up the road toward the public beach.

It was a hot, sticky morning, and Charlie was per-

spiring by the time he got to the beach. It certainly
didn't look as if it were going to rain to him. And lots
of other people must have felt the same way, too, he
decided, because the beach was already starting to get
crowded. Beach towels and blankets were scattered
everywhere, and bright umbrellas squatted on the
sand like giant toadstools. There were groups of
mothers sitting in clusters talking while they watched
their toddlers pat around in the wet sand near the
edge of the water. There were a number of castles
under construction and also some channels and
dammed-up pools. Farther up on the sand a young
couple lay with their arms around each other and their
eyes closed, and nearby an elderly gentleman in a
sand chair squinted at *The New York Times.*

Charlie trudged through the sand, keeping his
eyes peeled for some boys his own age. Then he saw
them. There must have been at least a dozen of them,
and they were playing volleyball up near the parking
lot. Charlie broke into a run. It should be easy to get
into the game, he thought.

He stopped a few feet from where the boys were
jumping and hollering as they punched the ball back
and forth across the high net. They seemed to be having a great time. Most of them looked about Charlie's
age or just a little older, and he held his breath waiting for a break in the game.

Just then from out of nowhere the volleyball
came smashing into Charlie's face, taking away his
breath and knocking him flat in the sand.

"Hey, Clod! That was a great play," someone
shouted.

Charlie lay there with his eyes closed, wishing

that the sand would open up and swallow him. He heard a burst of laughter from the others and then the shouting and stomping that told him they had forgotten all about him already and had gone back to their game.

Charlie got slowly to his feet, retrieved his towel and lunch sack, which he had dropped when he fell, and scuffed away, hoping that he would get lost in the crowd and never have to face those boys again.

After he had walked a few feet, he stopped and took the cyanide pill out of his lunch sack. He turned it over in his hand a few times and then popped it into his mouth. He wouldn't chew it up and swallow it, he decided. He would just let it melt. That way he would die slowly and tragically instead of just falling over in the sand the way he had when the volleyball smacked him in the face. Maybe then the boys would think that he died of a concussion and be sorry that they had laughed.

Charlie was so busy picturing how he was going to die that he scarcely noticed that a sea gull had fluttered down from the sky and landed beside him. When he suddenly realized that the sea gull was walking along with him, he nearly choked on his cyanide pill and accidentally spit it into the sand. Charlie stopped. The bird stopped. Then Charlie took three steps. The bird strutted up to where he stood and stopped beside him.

This time Charlie was not afraid, even though he was sure that this was the same bird that he had seen the day before. This was no evil spirit. It was a friend.

Charlie spread his towel on the sand and sat down. As if on cue, the gull lowered its feathered breast onto the warm sand, looking as if it were settling down to chat for a while. Charlie couldn't help but chuckle, and when he did, the bird cocked its head to one side and cooed softly. Charlie thought about saying something, but since he had never talked to a bird before (not even his grandmother's parakeet, even though she talked to it all the time), he just sat there feeling contented for the first time since he'd left home that morning.

After a while his stomach began to grumble, so he got out the peanut-butter-and-jelly sandwich that he had brought along for lunch. He broke off a corner of the sandwich and laid it in the sand beside the sea gull. The bird pecked at it every now and then while Charlie ate the rest.

Charlie was feeling very peaceful, and he didn't notice that the clouds were thickening and the sun had disappeared. Part of the time he was thinking about the sea gull, which still sat beside him, and the rest of the time he was absorbed in watching a man with a long-handled metal detector sweep back and forth across the sand. Every so often the man would bend down and dig in the sand until he pulled out whatever the machine had detected. Mostly he found matchbox cars and forgotten spoons from picnic lunches, but every once in a while he pulled up a quarter or a dime. Charlie wondered vaguely if the man had ever found anything really valuable, like a watch or a diamond ring.

Just as Charlie was pretending that the metal detector was a minesweeper and that the man was scanning the beach for hidden explosives, a bolt of lightning jackhammered across the sky, interrupting his dream.

All over the beach people began to scamper, gathering children and towels, and lowering umbrellas that were teetering in the sudden chilly wind. Charlie shivered and hugged his knees. He didn't want to leave as long as the sea gull stayed, but rain was making dime-size craters in the sand, and a moment later it came sweeping into shore in giant sheets, instantly soaking him to the skin.

Charlie jumped up and ran toward home. He looked back once, but the sea gull, too, had gone.

The storm did not let up all afternoon or evening, and the radio reported minor flooding in some areas along the beach. Charlie listened glumly to his sister and mother talk about clothes all through supper, and then he excused himself and went to his room.

He flopped across his bed and drifted off to sleep, lulled by the sound of rain drumming against his windows. A moment later Charlie was in the tunnel again, the long, black tunnel, and there at the end was the same flickering fire that he had seen the night before.

CHAPTER 3

CHARLIE COULD no longer hear the sounds of the storm. He was aware of nothing except the beautiful scarlet flames, like beckoning fingers that burned before his eyes. He did not move, but the fire seemed to float toward him, bringing with it a delicious warmth.

The fire came closer and closer, until Charlie could see that it was burning in an old-fashioned type of fireplace, the kind his mother always called a hearth. He could not see the hearth clearly at first because the fire was still too far away, but gradually it moved closer and closer and then stopped no more than a dozen feet from his bed. The reflection of the flames played merrily on the hearthstone, and above it the outline of the stone chimney was visible in the soft glow.

Suddenly the fire changed. The flames seemed to jump faster and higher, as if they were a hundred frantic hands reaching for some prize suspended above them in the chimney. The sound, which had been a soft *whoosh* at first, was now a roar that was sharply punctuated by crackling wood. As the fire grew more intense, the light that came from it grew brighter, too, so that Charlie could finally see the entire fireplace, and he let out a low whistle of disbelief.

The chimney was made out of common field-stones from floor to ceiling, except for one stone in the center, just above the opening. It was a flat, rectangular stone about four feet high, with a rounded top, and words and figures had been carved into its face.

"It's a gravestone," Charlie whispered. His scalp began to tingle. He couldn't see it clearly enough to read the words, but that didn't matter. Charlie knew that they spelled the name of someone, someone who was dead.

"I want to wake up!" he shouted, but his words were lost in the roar of the fire, which was growing larger and larger until the hearth could barely contain it.

As the fire grew brighter, Charlie could see that he was not in a tunnel after all. He was in a room, but before he could look around the room, his attention was drawn back to the fire. It had grown so enormous that the chimney could not draw off all of the smoke. It billowed out into the room, swirling around him, choking him and making him cough.

I've got to get out of here, Charlie thought frantically, but the smoke was so thick that he could not find the door. He tried to stop coughing so that he would not use up what precious oxygen there was left in the room, but the smoke was hurting his nose and throat and making his lungs ache, and he could not stop.

I'm only dreaming, Charlie reasoned. All that I have to do is wake up. The next instant he opened his eyes. The dream was gone. The room was dark.

Charlie buried his face in his pillow and coughed deeply. His chest throbbed and his eyes stung.

Charlie sat up quickly. Why was he coughing if it was just a dream? Smoke! He could smell it. Was it real? Or was he still dreaming?

Suddenly the baseboard in the center of the wall opposite his bed burst into flame. Charlie blinked his eyes and looked again, but a tiny match-size flame was moving slowly up the wall, fanning out slightly as it rose.

Charlie watched hypnotically, unable to move, as the fire reached a height of about three feet and then stopped spreading. It crackled and spat merrily just as the fire had done in Charlie's dream.

There was a commotion in the hallway and Mrs. Potter burst into the room. She stopped, looking first at the fire and then at Charlie, as if she couldn't believe her eyes. Stumbling back into the hallway, she shouted for Nanabelle to call the fire department.

Charlie sank back against the headboard of his bed and watched the delicate flames caress the wall, feeling as if he were in a trance.

A moment later his mother was back. Water sloshed out of the bathroom wastebasket in her hands, and she tossed it quickly on the fire.

When the water hit, the flames hissed and sputtered and were lost in a veil of white smoke. The spell was broken.

Just then Nanabelle came tearing into the room with more speed than Charlie could remember ever seeing her display.

"Charlie! Are you all right?" she cried. Then

she stopped and stared at the blackened spot on the wall. "What on earth!"

Mrs. Potter was on her knees, poking at the charred wall. "Must have started in the wiring," she said. "It seems to be out, but we'll all sleep a lot better when the fire department looks it over."

"Let's go down and make some coffee," said Nanabelle in a shaky voice. "Coming, Charlie?"

"Naw," he said with a shrug.

Charlie was glad when they had left him alone again, and he stared at the spot where the fire had burned. Maybe there was a secret passage behind that wall that led to one of the other houses along the beach. And maybe whoever lived in the other house had sneaked through the secret passage and set fire in his room because they knew that he was a secret agent.

Charlie sighed. The fire hadn't started in any secret passage. It hadn't started in the wiring, either. He knew that. It had started in his dream in a fireplace with a gravestone in the center. It had been coming closer and closer, trying to reach him. Charlie shivered.

Now it was here.

CHAPTER 4

AS THE wail of the fire engine grew louder, Charlie thought about how disappointed the firemen would be when they got to his house and discovered that the fire was already out. When he was younger, he had imagined that he was a fireman hundreds of times. And he had always jumped ten stories into the net at the last possible moment before the building collapsed, and he had always carried a scared little kid in his arms. He knew how disappointed he would have been if he had gotten there after the fire was already out.

A moment later the engine stopped in front of the house, and the siren made a pitiful moaning sound as it died away.

Charlie went to the top of the stairs and listened as his mother opened the door and explained to the firemen about the fire.

"Sounds like we'd better take a look," he heard one of the firemen say.

Mrs. Potter led Nanabelle and two firemen up the stairs toward Charlie's room. The men were dressed in black rubber coats with wide yellow stripes around the middle, tall boots, and wide-brimmed fire hats. Both men nodded hello as they passed Charlie, and he nodded back and followed them into his room.

With a pounding heart he watched the firemen go over the entire wall with painstaking slowness, searching for hot spots that would indicate more fire. Charlie wished that he could tell the firemen about his dreams. Maybe they would be able to explain why he had had them. Maybe this kind of thing happened all the time, and he just didn't know about it. But deep down Charlie knew that that wasn't so and that the firemen would think that he was making up the dreams or that he had set the fire himself and was trying to weasel out of it, so he kept quiet.

One of the firemen was knocking on the wall with his fist. "There's something funny about this," he said. "I think that we'd better break open this wall."

"Go ahead, if that's what you have to do," said Mrs. Potter.

One of the firemen went to the truck and came back with an ax and two crowbars. Charlie fidgeted nervously. He didn't know what he expected them to find, but his heart kept right on pounding as he watched them work.

Plaster dust billowed as the two men picked at the hole they had made with the ax. Suddenly one of them stopped.

"This is too flimsy. I think it is a false wall. Probably some kind of partition. We'll know in a minute."

The fireman slipped his crowbar under part of the broken wall and jerked hard. A section nearly three feet square crumbled away. Charlie caught his breath. Through the dust he thought he could see a stone. And it looked like a flat rectangular stone with a rounded top.

"What in the world is that?" shrieked Nanabelle.

She sees it, too, thought Charlie. That proves that I'm not dreaming now.

One of the men shone his flashlight into the hole in the wall and peered inside.

"It's just an old fireplace," he said, turning toward Mrs. Potter.

Charlie held his breath, waiting for the man to notice the gravestone and point it out to Nanabelle and his mother. Maybe he hadn't noticed it himself, thought Charlie as the moments passed and the fireman said nothing, but that didn't seem very likely. The stone was over three feet high and set squarely in the center of the chimney. The only other possibility that he could think of was that the fireman did not want to alarm the women. Charlie thought about that for a moment and decided that must be the answer. He wondered if he should make some sign to the firemen to show he knew that the gravestone was there, too, and that he would be cool and very helpful if his mother and Nanabelle should become hysterical. But before he could devise a sign, the men turned back to the wall.

"Better keep back," one of them said. "I want to finish pulling this wall down, so that we can get a better look."

Mrs. Potter grabbed Charlie's hand and squeezed it so hard that he nearly yelped. "If only your father were here," she mumbled.

Before Charlie could think up any words of comfort for his mother, there was a large crash as another section of the wall gave way. Nanabelle threw open the windows as plaster dust quickly engulfed the room and everyone began to cough.

As soon as the dust had cleared, the men picked up their crowbars again. "I'm sorry about all this dust. Maybe you'd rather wait in another room until we're finished."

Charlie shook his head quickly. He couldn't leave. He had to know at the first possible moment if this fireplace really was the same one that he had seen in his dreams. Neither Mrs. Potter nor Nanabelle made any move to leave, either, so the men went back to their work.

The last section of wall shuddered under the firemen's blows and then collapsed into a heap of broken plaster onto the floor.

Through the dust Charlie could make out the outline of the hearth. Gradually, as the air began to clear, he could see a large rectangular stone with a rounded top directly above the opening in the hearth. It *was* the same fireplace. There could be no doubt about it.

Charlie slumped onto his bed. He couldn't believe that this was really happening. Surely this was another dream, and any moment he would wake up. Until then, there was nothing to do but stare at the incredible gravestone. It was ornately carved from top to bottom, and just below the rounded top a pair of figures had been chiseled into the stone. One figure was a skeleton holding a scythe in one hand and a large candle snuffer in the other. The skeleton was preparing to snuff out a tall candle that stood between itself and the other figure, which was robed and winged and held an hourglass in its hand.

That's death! thought Charlie. The idea made him shiver, and he looked quickly down the face of the stone.

In Memory of
Abel Blacklaw
A Lad of 16 Years
Who Died a Wet and Slimy Death
In the Summer of 1712

Suddenly Mrs. Potter sneezed, and Charlie came back to life.

"Gesundheit!" he said quickly. His mother smiled and gazed toward the fireplace.

"What a lovely hearth," she mused. "I wonder why on earth anyone would want to board it up."

Charlie did a double take. In the squeamish department his mother was second only to Nanabelle, who, now that he noticed, was neither moaning nor looking as if she were going to throw up. Even the firemen didn't seem alarmed. What was wrong with everybody? Had they all gone blind?

Charlie quickly ran down the list of possibilities in his mind. It wasn't very likely that all four of them had gone blind at the exact same moment. Maybe he was seeing things himself. Maybe it was the power of suggestion brought on by his dreams. He had heard about things like that. Charlie blinked hard and looked at the gravestone again. But it was there, all right. There could be no doubt about it. He was sure that he wasn't dreaming, but he pinched himself just to be sure.

The last possibility was almost more than Charlie could bear to think. *He was the only person present who could see the gravestone over the hearth!* He wished desperately that the firemen would leave and that his mother and Nanabelle would go to bed so that he could be alone to inspect the stone. He needed to touch it and find out if it was just an illusion or if his fingers could actually feel the words carved into its face. It was impossible to believe that the fire had started there, and yet there was no other explanation. Then there were the dreams to be considered, too. It all had to be connected somehow, but he needed time to investigate if he was going to figure out how.

The firemen beamed their flashlights up the chimney and poked and prodded for a while longer and then announced that they were certain that the danger was over, although they weren't at all certain how the fire had started in the first place. Mrs. Potter seemed relieved even though she couldn't help adding one more time how she wished Mr. Potter were there.

Charlie watched with a growing sense of excitement, which his mother promptly dashed to pieces the moment the firemen were out the door.

"You can't possibly sleep in that room tonight," she said, steering him toward the spare bedroom. "With your sinuses and all that plaster dust everywhere, you'd sneeze yourself silly by morning."

All of his protests were in vain, so Charlie sighed, kissed his mother good night, and scuffed toward the spare bedroom in defeat. It was bad enough to be barred from his own room, but Charlie had a strong dislike for the spare bedroom, even though he had never slept there. The reason was because everything in it was exactly backward in relation to his own room.

The bed was on the opposite wall. The windows were in the opposite corners. Everything about it made him feel as if he had stepped through a mirror and were trapped on the inside.

Turning down the bed covers, Charlie sat on the edge of the bed. He tried to pretend that he was in a prisoner-of-war camp, but he couldn't concentrate. Besides, he thought, that's not nearly so exciting as having a fireplace made out of a gravestone right in your very own room.

Charlie knew that he had to sneak back into his room and investigate that gravestone. He could never go to sleep until he did, so he sat in the darkness until he was sure that his mother and Nanabelle had gone to bed. Then he went to the door and listened, but there was no sound anywhere. He swallowed hard, turned the knob, and tiptoed into the hall. The night light burning in the bathroom sent deep-red shadows spreading over the walls and floor. The door to his room was closed, and his pulse quickened as he slowly turned the knob and pushed it open.

"Psst," came a husky whisper from out of the darkness. "In with ye, matey, and latch the door behind thee!"

CHAPTER 5

THE BLOOD in Charlie's veins turned to ice. Had he really heard a voice? Or had it been his imagination? With a trembling hand he reached for the light switch just inside the door and flipped it on. Then, cautiously, he stuck his head in and peered around.

"Is anybody there?" he whispered.

The room was still. A soft snowfall of plaster dust had settled on every visible surface, and jagged pieces of wall were piled across the floor like rocky hills. A stuffed kangaroo stood frozen on the bed, and yesterday's shirt lay like a napping ghost across the chair. Towering above all this, in eerie contrast, was the smoke-darkened hearth with the figures of death carved into the center stone above it.

Tickly shivers raced up and down Charlie's backbone. He almost turned and ran, but since no one answered, he tiptoed into the room, telling himself that he was sneaking behind enemy lines.

The door had scarcely clicked shut when he heard a shuffle and then a voice.

"Well, that took long enough. Froze molasses woulda got here faster."

"Who's there?" demanded Charlie. "And where are you hiding?" It had to be someone playing a trick on him. After all, voices didn't come out of thin air. Maybe there really was a secret passageway between this house and one of the others along the beach. Maybe the other house belonged to one of the boys who had laughed at him at the volleyball game, and maybe the boy had decided to slip over and give Charlie a good scare.

"It's Abel Blacklaw, of course," the voice said a trifle impatiently. "And where would I be but over here admiring me gravestone. It's me calling card, and a handsome one at that, I'd say. Wouldn't you?"

Without answering, Charlie surveyed the room a second time. He knelt and looked beneath his bed, but all he saw was a rumpled pair of jeans and three sweat socks. There was no one in the closet, either, and the windows were closed and locked. Most puzzling of all was the fact that the floor was covered with plaster dust, and the only footprints were the ones that he had made searching for the intruder.

Charlie made a fist and punched his bed pillow in disgust, sending up clouds of dust to tickle his nose.

Peals of laughter danced through the air. "Hey, matey, ye ain't looked up the chimbley. Maybe I'm hanging up there by me fingers and toes."

Hairs stood out on the back of Charlie's neck like porcupine needles. As he scanned the room a third time, a terrible thought started forming in one of the wrinkles of his brain. Maybe it *was* possible. Maybe his dreams really had been caused by a ghost named Abel Blacklaw. Charlie shivered and read the words on the gravestone again. "Abel Blacklaw A Lad of 16 Years Who Died a Wet and Slimy Death In the Summer of 1712."

A wet and slimy death? Pictures of sunken ships and drowned corpses bobbed into Charlie's mind. Still, if he really was a ghost, he would have to be dealt with, so Charlie took a deep breath and said, "Then please come down where I can see you. It feels funny not knowing where to look when I talk."

Hearty laughter rang out once again. " 'Tis a sorry thing, matey, but I'm afraid I'm a bit hard to see."

That did it. The voice seemed to be coming from somewhere near the hearth, all right. Abel Blacklaw *was* hanging in the chimney, but in the shape of a tape recorder or a radio speaker instead of a ghost. Charlie smiled to himself. He had almost been fooled. But now he had the picture, and he was beginning to enjoy this prank. He hoped that it wouldn't be long until he met the person who was responsible for it. He was sure that they could become great friends.

Charlie sauntered casually toward the hearth. In a way he hated to end everything so soon by finding the tape recorder or speaker, but still, nothing could be so satisfying as the look on the prankster's face when Charlie called his bluff.

He stretched his arm as far up into the chimney as it would go and inched his hand across the bricks that lined it. Nothing. Then he went to his bureau and took a flashlight out of the bottom drawer. The beams made dull patterns as they twirled around the soot-caked chimney and dwindled away into darkness at the top. Still nothing. Hoisting one foot onto the hearthstone, he read again the words carved into the chimney and gave a puzzled sigh.

Suddenly something slapped him across the

shoulder, nearly knocking him off his feet. "Thought I was really up there, did ye, matey? Aye, you're a good one for a joke, ye are. I can see we're gonna have great times."

Charlie whirled around in the empty room. Like it or not, he was being attacked by an invisible enemy. He started inching slowly toward the door.

"Don't leave, matey," said the voice, which had become soft and cajoling now. "Bile me in oil and I wouldn't hurt ye. Ye have me honest word on that."

Charlie halted his retreat. He had to admit that the ghost of Abel Blacklaw didn't sound very menacing. Still, he couldn't give in too easily.

"Then what do you want?" challenged Charlie.

From somewhere near the hearth Abel Blacklaw chuckled softly. Then, as Charlie watched in amazement, a handful of plaster dust rose from the floor near where the voice had seemed to come from. It swirled around and around until it formed an eddy that wheeled and whirled about the room like a runaway top. After a moment the funnel crumbled and the pale dust trickled back to the floor, but the lively breeze that had propelled it twirled on, rippling book pages on Charlie's desk, fanning the hem of a curtain, and raising so much dust that he began to sneeze. Charlie sneezed until his eyes were watering. "What are you trying to do to me, you stupid ghost?" he said choking.

Before Abel Blacklaw could answer, there was a rustling in the hall. The door opened and Mrs. Potter leaned wearily into the room. "Charlie? Is that you?" she said, clutching her bathrobe and squinting in the light.

"Uh . . . yeah, Mom," said Charlie. He struggled to hold back another sneeze and prayed silently that his invisible guest would behave himself and not scare the living daylights out of his mother.

"Well, what in the name of good sense are you doing?" Mrs. Potter demanded. "You'll wake up the dead with all the racket you're making!"

Charlie couldn't be sure, but he thought he heard Abel Blacklaw snicker.

"I couldn't sleep, so I thought I'd take another look at the fireplace." Charlie said the words loudly, hoping to cover up any sounds the ghost might make.

"Shhhhhhh!" his mother shushed him crossly. "Now get back to bed and get some sleep. Let the rest of us get some sleep, too. I just hope you don't have nightmares now and keep me awake the rest of the night." With that she stomped off down the hall.

"Okay, Mom. I'll go in a minute," Charlie called after her. When he was sure she was back in her room he looked around for signs of Abel Blacklaw, but the dust had all settled again and there were no telltale whirlpools of air dancing around the room.

"Abel?" he whispered. "Are you still here?"

"Aye, matey. Here I be."

"I have to go now. Mom'll throw a fit if I stay in here any longer. But you still didn't tell me what you want or where you came from, for that matter."

"So I didn't, matey." The ghost paused, and when he spoke again his voice had a deadly serious ring. "But how do I know I can trust thee? Eh?"

"Trust me? Of course you can trust me. Besides, what could I do to you, anyway?"

Abel Blacklaw laughed softly, and when he spoke his voice was friendly again. "Of course I can trust thee, matey. Never have I met a lad with a truer heart."

Charlie felt a weight behind his neck, like an arm being draped around his shoulders. "Now here's what you do," whispered the ghost into Charlie's left ear. "Tommorrow night get thyself down to the beach as soon as it's dark. Go to the spot just beneath the seawall and wait for me there."

Charlie swallowed down a lump that was growing in his throat. "Yes, sir. I'll be there."

"Aye. That's a good lad," said the ghost, removing his invisible arm from Charlie's shoulders. Charlie moved toward the door.

"There's one more thing that I forgot to tell ye," said the voice beside the hearth. "There's something you'll be having to fetch."

"What's that?"

Abel Blacklaw's voice was serious again. "A skull!" he whispered hoarsely.

Charlie's heart lurched. "What!"

"Aye, matey. I'll be needing a skull wrapped in black cloth and a long, sharp quill for writing in blood."

Peals of ghostly laughter echoed about the room. Beside the hearth an eddy of dust was forming again, growing bigger and bigger. The whirlpool grew until it was taller than Charlie, hanging in the air just above the floor. Suddenly, as if sucked up by a giant vacuum cleaner, it whooshed up the chimney and was gone, taking the echoing laughter with it as it went.

CHAPTER 6

CHARLIE LAY awake in the darkness in the spare bedroom for a long time thinking about Abel Black-law. There was no doubt about it—he was a genuine, bona-fide ghost, and whatever purpose had made him appear, he had apparently decided to make Charlie part of it, whether Charlie liked it or not.

The more he thought about it, the more he did like it after all. It sure was better than playing army all alone. The only thing that worried him was the skull and quill-for-writing-in-blood part. He couldn't help wondering if that had been another one of Abel's jokes. Surely he didn't expect Charlie to be able to come up with a real skull.

The next morning Charlie had to drag himself out of bed. His lack of sleep had left him feeling as if he had been run over by a tank. His arms and legs were almost too heavy to move, and there was a dull throb just behind his eyes. He struggled into his clothes and went downstairs hoping breakfast would revive him.

He hadn't counted on having to face Nanabelle across the table, but there she sat, looking as if she had been dead for at least three days.

"Well, if it isn't my little brother, the pyro-maniac," she said in a voice dripping with sarcasm.

"Nanabelle!" said Mrs. Potter before Charlie could think up an appropriate answer. "Good morning, dear," she added without looking around from where she stood at the stove cooking eggs.

"Oh, really, Mom. The little monster had to have been playing with matches. Surely you don't think that fire started all by itself inside a fireplace that had been boarded up for years!"

Charlie stuck his tongue out at his sister and poured himself a glass of milk. "Good morning, Mom," he said in a superangelic voice that made Nanabelle look as if she were going to throw up.

"I still say it started in the wiring," said Mrs. Potter. "I certainly know that Charlie wouldn't try to burn down the house around us, and I'm very disturbed at you for insinuating such a thing, Nanabelle."

Mrs. Potter turned and slid a plate of scrambled eggs and bacon in front of Nanabelle. "What would you like to eat this morning, Charlie? Scrambled eggs and bacon?"

"Sounds great," he said, giving his mother his best smile.

Mrs. Potter turned around again to resume her cooking, and Nanabelle made a face at Charlie.

"I certainly must say that is a lovely fireplace," said his mother. "I can't imagine why anybody would want to board it up."

Nanabelle was ignoring him now, concentrating on her breakfast. Charlie drained his glass of milk and sat back in his chair waiting for his breakfast and half listening to his mother ramble on about the fire. Suddenly a movement on the counter caught his attention.

Charlie blinked and looked at the open egg carton, where a large white egg was rising slowly in the air. Nobody else saw it, and Charlie stared in fascination as it floated across the room. An instant later his fascination turned to horror. The egg stopped and hovered in midair for a few seconds, right above Nanabelle, and then dropped with a *splot!* on her head.

Nanabelle jumped up with a shriek as the slimy egg ran through her hair and down her face.

"Charlie Potter! You miserable brat! I'm going to kill you for this!" she screamed, turning to her astonished mother. "Look! He threw an egg at me!"

"I did *not*," Charlie sputtered. "How could I? I was just sitting here all the time!"

"I don't know how you did it, but you *did it!*" Nanabelle cried, lunging at Charlie as if she were going to choke him.

Mrs. Potter stepped between them. Her face was clouded with rage. "Charles Winston Potter," she said angrily. "What is the meaning of this?"

"I didn't do it," Charlie insisted. "I would have had to get up and walk across the room and get an egg. You would have seen me or heard me if I had done that." He looked helplessly first at his mother and then at Nanabelle, who was making a horrible face and wiping egg yolk out of her hair with a paper napkin.

"Well, *I* certainly didn't throw it," said Mrs. Potter. "And I'm sure Nanabelle didn't throw it at herself. So just what other possible explanation could there be?"

Charlie could feel his face turning red. He was trapped. He would either have to take the blame for it himself or tell them about the ghost of Abel Blacklaw. That would scare the wits out of them, *if* they believed him, which they probably wouldn't. The thought made him chuckle, so he said in his best Boris Karloff voice, "It was the ghost of Abel Blacklaw."

Nanabelle let out a bloodcurdling scream and ran out of the room. Mrs. Potter's eyes widened for an instant and then hardened into cold anger. Charlie cringed under her sharp gaze and waited for her to speak. She had three speeches that she always used when she got angry at him, and he vaguely wondered if it would be number one—"I don't know what I'm going to do with you," or number two—"Wait until your father gets here this weekend," or number three —"You're going to have to be punished for this."

"I don't know what I'm going to do with you," said Mrs. Potter.

Charlie breathed a sigh of relief. Number one was reserved for minor crimes and usually amounted to nothing more than a bawling out.

"I just don't understand all this bickering and fighting that goes on between the two of you all the time," Mrs. Potter went on. She turned back to the stove and scooped a sizable portion of scrambled eggs onto the plate, added two slices of bacon and two pieces of buttered toast, and set the plate in front of Charlie. "You're brother and sister, not mortal enemies. I would think that you would have a little love and respect for each other."

Charlie said a weak "Yes, ma'am," and attacked the pile of food on his plate, thinking that he did have a little love and respect for Nanabelle, but very little. It was her own fault for acting so drippy all the time.

He finished his breakfast and left the kitchen, escaping just as Nanabelle reentered the room with her nose in the air and a bath towel wrapped around her hair. Back in the spare bedroom, he sprawled across the bed to plan a course of action for the day. He decided that the first order of business would be to find a skull. But where? Skulls weren't the sort of things that you found just lying around.

He flopped over onto his back and gazed at the ceiling. His science teacher back in Poughkeepsie had an entire skeleton on a stand in his classroom, but that wouldn't do Charlie much good here. Midnight scenes of secret grave robbings flickered ghoulishly in his mind and made him shiver. "I'm certainly not going to go out and rob any grave," Charlie thought resolutely. "Hey, wait a minute. Abel Blacklaw would know more about skulls than I do." The thought made Charlie shiver again, and he jumped and looked around the room.

"Abel, are you here?" he demanded. There was no sound and not so much as a ripple of a breeze in response. He went to the door, opened it a crack, and peered into the hall. The coast was clear. Hurrying to his own bedroom, he slipped inside. Everything looked the same as when he had left it the night before.

"Abel, are you here?" he asked in a husky whisper. Still there was no response. Charlie waited a moment and then went to the fireplace. Cupping his hands around his mouth, he called softly up the chimney, "Abel, where are you? I need you."

Again the ghost did not answer. Charlie scowled

at Abel Blacklaw's name carved into the gravestone. First Abel got him into trouble by dropping an egg on Nanabelle's head, and now, when he could be of some help, he was nowhere to be found.

Slipping out of the room and down the stairs, Charlie tiptoed through the hall and out the door before Nanabelle could spot him and start harassing him again or his mother could send him off to do some chore.

The sun felt warm, and he ambled down toward the beach. The tide was high, leaving only a narrow strip of sand between the water and the seawall. Charlie walked along the sand looking out across the water. Maybe the Sound would wash up a skull and leave it sticking up out of the sand at low tide. The thought made him shudder. A few steps farther he came across a long white sea-gull feather resting on the sand. He walked past it and then backed up. It would make a perfect quill for writing in blood. He could trim it with his pocketknife when he got back to his room.

Charlie stuck the feather into his back pants pocket and ambled on. When he reached the spot beside the seawall where he had arranged to meet Abel Blacklaw at dusk, he sat down in the sand and began to ponder his dilemma. Even though he had a quill for writing in blood, there was absolutely, positively no place he knew of where he could get a skull. Abel Blacklaw had said that he must bring one, and there was a chance that without it Abel would never reveal the secret of where he had come from and why he was here.

Charlie had to know the answers to these questions. Maybe the ghost was going to unleash something sinister) Maybe he was plotting to unlease it on the whole country, or, worse yet, on the whole world, and he, Charlie Potter, would miss the chance to save the whole human race if he did not know what it was. Charlie sank back against the seawall. He had to admit that his ghostly friend did not seem to be all that sinister. Nevertheless, he knew that he could not take the chance. He had to find a skull. But where?

Charlie sat there thinking about his problem until his stomach told him that it was lunchtime. Sneaking into the house, he tiptoed past the door to the living room, where Nanabelle was jumping around in her black leotard and tights, with the stereo turned full blast. Upstairs he could hear the vacuum cleaner going in his room, which pinpointed the location of his mother. His timing had been perfect, and he slipped into the kitchen, concocted two peanut-butter-and-jelly sandwiches, and slipped out of the house again.

Back at the beach, he quickly devoured the two sandwiches. The first one was delicious, but the second one was slightly gritty from having been dropped in the sand.

Wading in the water, Charlie decided that he was tired of thinking about Abel Blacklaw and the skull. He had been thinking about the skull all morning and had not made one single bit of progress, except for finding a quill for writing in blood. Casting a longing glance toward the public beach, a plan began to form in his mind. It was dull and boring and lonely on the private beach, and there was nothing to do in the house. If he stayed close to the seawall, he would be out of sight of his house, and his mother would never know it if he sneaked off to the forbidden public beach. He had gotten away with it once. Surely he could do it again.

Charlie moved stealthily along the private beaches, most of which were posted against trespassers. He was on a secret mission to recover the corpse of a slain American spy. "Just be sure that you bring back his skull," Charlie's commanding officer had ordered, "because the intelligence is hidden in a filling in one of his teeth." Charlie crouched low behind a sand dune as a squadron of sea gulls—enemy bombers—came diving out of the sky to strafe the beach. The sea gulls veered away and Charlie stood up again, breathing a sigh of relief. They had not seen him.

Suddenly a hand clamped down on his shoulder, and Charlie froze.

CHAPTER 7

"YOU DEAF, son?" boomed a hearty voice.

I'm caught, thought Charlie. Caught trespassing on a private beach. The hand released his shoulder and Charlie turned slowly to face his captor.

"I called to you three or four times." To Charlie's surprise, the man who was speaking was smiling, and Charlie had the fleeting feeling that he had seen him before. Then Charlie noticed an object in the man's hand. It was a long-handled metal detector, and this was the man Charlie had watched as he swept the beach the day before. "Thought maybe you could use some company," the man said.

"Sure," said Charlie, falling into step beside the stranger. In spite of his scare, Charlie liked this tall, lank man whose lazy, toothy smile hung like a sagging clothesline between large, pointed ears.

"Ever see one of these before?" he asked, nodding toward the metal detector in his hand.

"Nope," said Charlie. "I just saw yours yesterday."

"Well," the man mused. "If I was to know a fellow's name, I might just be willing to show him how it works."

"You would?" gasped Charlie. Then, remember-

46

ing his manners, he said, "I'm Charles Potter, sir. But you can call me Charlie."

"Well, Charlie, it's a real pleasure to meet you," the man said, reaching out his empty hand and shaking Charlie's hand vigorously. "My name's John Bobatoon, but you can call me Fixin' John. Folks call me that because fixin's my business. Why, there's nothing made that I can't fix. 'If it can be broken, I can fix it.' That's my motto."

Charlie looked up at Fixin' John with growing admiration, thinking how his own attempts to fix things usually ended in disaster. His admiration must have shown in his face because Fixin' John winked one eye at him and said, "The trick to fixin' is believin'. You're never going to get anything to work if you don't *believe* it'll work."

Charlie thought back to last summer, when he had believed that he could fix his father's power mower. He had believed that he could make it work right up to the time that he got all of the parts spread out on the garage floor. Then, he had to admit, he had lost his faith.

When they reached the public beach, Fixin' John handed Charlie a pair of earphones and told him to put them on. Eagerly Charlie obeyed. If only Henry and his other friends back in Poughkeepsie could see him now.

'This is the search coil," said Fixin' John. He was pointing toward an object on the lower end of the rod that looked very much like an inverted pie plate. "It sends an electromagnetic field into the ground. If that field is disturbed by metal, it registers a signal that you'll hear through the earphones."

Charlie nodded that he understood and looked longingly at the metal detector, which Fixin' John still held. At the top of the rod was a small box that Charlie decided must contain the electrical circuits. Fixin' John pushed a button on the side of a box and handed the unit to Charlie. Just as Charlie grasped the rod with both hands, a soft sound came through the earphones. Beep . . . beep . . . beep . . .

"Fixin' John! I've got something!" he shouted, nearly dropping the metal detector in his excitement.

Fixin' John smiled broadly. "Take it easy, son. Those beeps just let you know it's working. Now listen to this."

Fishing a nickel out of his pocket, Fixin' John stubbed it into the sand until it was out of sight. "Pass the rod over that," he instructed.

Charlie swung the detector in the direction of the buried nickel. As he got closer to the coin, the speed of the beeps increased until, when he was directly over it, they were an almost constant drone.

Charlie beamed a big smile up at Fixin' John, who nodded in return, picked up the nickel, and motioned for Charlie to continue sweeping the beach.

Gripping the rod tightly, Charlie concentrated mind and muscle on the task ahead. It was up to him to lead his platoon to safety across the mine-infested beachhead. One slip and he and his men would be blown to smithereens. The beeps coming from the minesweeper were slow and steady now. Inhaling deeply, he inched a foot across the sand. Beep . . . beep . . . beep . . . Over the sounds of the beeps he could hear aircraft, but he dared not look up to see if it was friend or foe.

Beep . . . beep . . . beep . . . Perspiration ran down his face in rivers and he squinted ahead, but there was nothing visible aboveground to give away the locations of the deadly mines. Beep . . . beep . . . beep . . . Suddenly the tempo quickened. Charlie froze. The minesweeper was slightly to the right of the path. With the coolness expected of an officer, Charlie extended the sweeper farther to the right.

The beeps continued to accelerate. Beep . . . beep . . . beep . . . Charlie's heartbeat accelerated, too, beating even faster than the beeps from his machine. He tensed and listened. Beep . . beep . . beep . beep . beepbeepbeepbeepbeep. . . .

Charlie moved the machine to the left again and observed the spot where the beeps had been the fastest. He turned off the sweeper, set it down in the sand, and gingerly approached his objective.

He had lost his bayonet in an earlier skirmish, so, under the watchful eyes of his men, Charlie dug a trembling finger into the sand. He flinched as he touched a smooth surface. He would have to be careful not to set off the mine himself. Taking a deep breath, he probed the sand again. Out of the corner of his eye, he could see his second-in-command, Sergeant Fixin' John, bending close to watch the operation.

His finger brushed the object a second time. Steadying himself, he pushed his whole hand into the sand. He had found something, all right, but whatever it was, it wasn't a mine. He ran his hand around what seemed to be a small cylinder and then carefully extracted it from the spot where it was buried.

Charlie caught his breath. He could not believe his eyes. In his hand he held a vial of deadly nerve gas,

the same gas that he had searched the beach for only
the day before.

As Charlie stared at the vial Sergeant Fixin'
John began to chuckle beside him. "Too bad your
first find was something worthless," he said.

Charlie blinked and looked at the empty spray
can of suntan lotion in his hand. "Yeah," he said
with a shrug. He hoped that Fixin' John had not noticed that he had been dreaming.

Giving Charlie a sympathetic look, Fixin' John
sighed and said, "Guess I had better have it back now,
son. I've got a lot of beach to sweep before dark."

"Sure," said Charlie. "And thanks."

"Tell you what," said Fixin' John, draping an
arm around Charlie's shoulder in a fatherly fashion.
"I'm here every afternoon about this time. Whenever
you feel like trying it again, you just hunt me up.
Okay?"

Charlie smiled at Fixin' John, saying that he
would, and started for home. It was getting late and
his mother would be wondering where he was.

He hoped that Fixin' John had really meant it
when he said that Charlie could use the metal detector
again. Using it had been just about the most fun of
anything that had happened since he left Poughkeepsie, except, of course, for Abel Blacklaw. But
Charlie wasn't sure yet, at least, if having a ghost was
going to turn out to be a good experience or a terrible
one.

Suddenly Charlie stopped dead still in his tracks.
The skull! Of course! Why hadn't he thought of it before? Breaking into a run, Charlie hurried across the
sand toward home.

CHAPTER 8

CHARLIE NEARLY burst with excitement as he bounded toward the house. If it hadn't been for Fixin' John and the minesweeper and the vial of deadly nerve gas, he would never have thought of it. And it was so simple, too. His army-surplus gas mask would make a perfect skull. Now, with the sea-gull feather for a quill for writing in blood and his gas mask for a skull, all he would have to do was wait for darkness to come and he would meet the ghost of Abel Blacklaw at the seawall.

In spite of the warm summer sun, Charlie shivered with anticipation as he crossed the sweeping back lawn and opened the door. His plan was to go directly to his room, find the skull, and get everything ready for the secret rendezvous that night. His plan was abruptly changed by a voice from the kitchen.

"Hello, son. How did your week go?"

Charlie blinked at his father in bewilderment. He had lost all track of the days and hadn't even realized that it was Saturday, the day his father came down from Poughkeepsie. What made matters even worse was the fact that Saturday nights were always family nights. Everybody sat around the supper table for an extra long time talking about what had happened

51

during the week. Then they would all go into the living room and play cards or checkers or Monopoly until bedtime. Sometimes they even popped corn to eat while they played. Charlie's heart sank into his shoes.

"Well, son. Aren't you even going to say hello?"

"Oh, sure, Dad. *Hello!* I mean, well, you just surprised me, that's all." Charlie felt his face flush and knew that he was getting himself in deeper and deeper, but he just couldn't stop talking. "You see, I forgot that you come down on Saturday. I mean, I know that you come down on Saturday. It's just that I was surprised that it got to be Saturday so fast. I mean . . . well, you know what I mean."

"Yes. I'm afraid so," said Mr. Potter. Charlie winced as he detected a slight note of impatience in his father's voice.

"I'm sure glad to see you, Dad. *Really* I am," called Charlie as he bounded up the stairs two at a time. When he opened the door to his own room, the plaster dust had been vacuumed away and everything was neat and tidy again. Only the gravestone, which only Charlie could see, and the hearth were left as silent reminders of the strange events that had occurred there the night before.

Rummaging around in the back of his closet, Charlie soon found his army-surplus gas mask. If that doesn't look like a skull, nothing does, he thought as he held it up for inspection. Now to wrap it in a black cloth, he mused. Charlie had temporarily forgotten about the black-cloth part, and now he suddenly realized that he had nothing that would do. His underwear was white, his jeans were blue, and his shirts were every color in the world but black. He sat down on the edge of the bed and thought about the problem.

After a while he remembered the linen closet in the hall, but a quick inspection failed to uncover either black towels or black sheets. He was just about to go back to his room when an object in Nanabelle's room caught his attention. There, lying crumpled on the floor, was the black leotard that she had been wearing to cavort around the living room earlier that day.

No one was around, so Charlie darted into Nanabelle's room, snatched up the leotard, and hightailed it for his own room before anyone could come upstairs and catch him. Then he stuffed the skull inside the leotard, wrapped it into a tight bundle, and hid it under his bed along with the quill for writing in blood. Now the only problem that remained was how to escape to the beach.

Conversation at the supper table all centered around the fire of the night before and the hearth that it had uncovered.

"There's certainly something suspicious about the whole thing," said Mr. Potter, who had inspected the fireplace immediately upon his arrival at the beach house. Out of the corner of his eye, Charlie could see Nanabelle smirking at him, victory shining in her eyes.

"On the other hand," Mr. Potter went on, "I can't see any way it could have started *except* in the wiring."

Charlie returned Nanabelle's smirk, and she looked away in disgust.

"What do you have to say about the whole thing, Charlie?" asked his father. "After all, it happened in your room."

Nanabelle was smirking again. Charlie tried to ignore her and shrugged. "I was sound asleep when it started. The smoke woke me up," he said.

"A likely story," Nanabelle muttered. Then, getting no response, she said in a braver voice, "If you ask me, *someone* was probably playing with matches."

"Well, if you're going to play with matches, at least do it in your own room," said Charlie grinning triumphantly.

"All right, you two!" interjected Mrs. Potter. "I think it's time we changed the subject."

Charlie turned to his roast beef while Nanabelle began describing in great detail all the new school clothes that she had acquired during the week. His mind was at work again trying to come up with a plan of escape, but try as he might, he could not think of a single possibility.

Suddenly Charlie noticed a slight movement just behind Nanabelle's left shoulder. He laid his fork on the edge of his plate and watched in fascination as a long strand of her hair twined itself around a rung in the ladder-back chair in which she sat. In one slow, smooth motion, the strand of hair wound in and out until it had formed a perfect square knot around the rung of the chair. Charlie cringed as he realized what was happening. Abel Blacklaw was at it again.

Picking up his fork, Charlie speared a piece of roast beef and put it into his mouth, but he could barely force himself to chew. Voices droned unintelligibly around him, but his total concentration was on that knot of hair and what would happen when Nanabelle stood up.

Charlie took a deep breath and began counting

the peas on his plate. He had to do something to get his mind off Nanabelle's hair. There was nothing that he could do about the situation except let it happen, and he knew that as long as he had it on his mind, he would also have a guilty look on his face.

Suppertime went on forever. He could not remember ever having sat through such a long meal. Charlie stared into his plate. He had scarcely touched his food. But how could he eat? Any minute now a pair of guards would unlock his cell and step inside. "Is it time?" he would ask, already knowing the answer. They would nod silently, and he would stand up on shaking legs. Then he would square his shoulders and try to look brave as he left his cell and made that last, long walk down the corridor toward the electric chair.

Suddenly Charlie's dream was punctuated by a scream. It was Nanabelle, and she was standing half bent over the chair around which her hair was firmly knotted. She was screaming her head off and pointing straight at him.

For the next few minutes chaos reigned supreme. Nanabelle alternated between shrieking in pain and hurling accusations at Charlie. Mrs. Potter hovered nearby, gingerly trying to loosen the knot in Nanabelle's hair, and Mr. Potter stomped back and forth across the room shouting things like "What in the world is going on around here?" and "This isn't a beach house. It's a *mad*house!" to no one in particular. Only Charlie remained too stunned to move or utter a sound.

He had an idea of what was coming next, and he was right. At the exact same moment that Nanabelle's hair was untied from the chair, all eyes turned to Charlie.

"How could I have done it? I've been sitting here all the time," he begged. "You would have seen me."

"You conniving little brat," Nanabelle shouted. "I don't know how you did it, but you *did* it!"

"How *did* you do it, Charlie?" asked Mr. Potter, looking genuinely puzzled.

Charlie looked helplessly from one angry face to the other. He was trapped. There was no way that he could convince them he was innocent, but at the same time there was no way to explain how it had happened, either.

"Charlie, your father asked you a question," Mrs. Potter said gravely.

Charlie scrunched down in his chair and began counting the peas on his plate again. Still he did not answer.

"All right, son," said Mr. Potter in a stern voice. "If that's your attitude, then you can go to your room for the rest of the evening. No Saturday-night fun for you!"

Charlie eased sideways out of his chair and with one last helpless glance at his mother trudged sadly toward his room. Only after he had closed the door and flopped across his bed did he realize what had happened.

He was free! The maple tree outside his bedroom window would make a perfect escape route, and no one would even know that he was gone.

CHAPTER 9

CHARLIE SAT crosslegged in the sand beside the seawall, idly tapping his flashlight against the sole of his shoe and watching the lights of a tanker move across the dark horizon like an earthbound constellation. The skull wrapped in black cloth rested on his lap, and the quill for writing in blood was stuck firmly behind his left ear. He was ready, but it had been dark for a full fifteen minutes and there was no sign that the ghost of Abel Blacklaw was anywhere nearby.

He slapped at a mosquito on his arm and wondered for the umpteenth time if he should forget the whole thing and sneak back to his room. At best, Abel Blacklaw was a strange one. Maybe agreeing to meet him here had been a mistake.

Nervously Charlie looked up and down the beach. He was alone. Even the sea gulls were gone for the night, and the rising tide crashed noisily against the sandy shore above the pounding of his heart.

Still, he thought, if Abel had wanted to harm him, he had had plenty of other chances. With a little luck, this could turn out to be the greatest adventure of his whole life.

Charlie flicked on the flashlight and put the

luminous end under his chin so that the beam flared upward over his face. Grinning his most ghostly grin, he started speaking in his Boris Karloff voice: "This is Charles Winston Potter calling the ghost of Abel Blacklaw." He paused. A shiver tiptoed up his spine. "I have brought a skull wrapped in black cloth and a quill for . . ."

Suddenly from somewhere above him Charlie heard the rush of wings, like a sea gull swooping down from the sky. He ducked as the next word froze on his lips. Switching off the flashlight, he sat trembling in the sudden blackness.

By the time his eyes had adjusted to the dark, the bird or animal or whatever had made the sound was gone. Charlie decided not to wait around any longer. Gathering up his flashlight, the skull wrapped in black cloth, and the quill, he stood up in the sand.

Just then a voice sounded from somewhere to his right. "Hey, matey. You aren't packing off to go, now, are ye? I bloody well just got here!"

Charlie gulped and looked in the direction from which the voice had come, but his mysterious friend was as invisible as ever.

"I got tired of waiting," said Charlie. "Besides, I thought you weren't going to show."

The night air rang with laughter. "You've got a lot to learn about Abel Blacklaw, matey. A *lot* to learn."

"Yes, sir," said Charlie, thinking to himself that that was just about the biggest dose of truth he had heard in a long time.

Abel's voice was sober when he spoke again.

"Time's a-wasting! Bring your torch up closer to the wall."

Charlie's brow wrinkled in a puzzled frown. "Torch?" he asked.

"That thing you was lighting your face up with," said Abel impatiently. "If that's not a torch, then what be it?"

"Oh, that. That's a flashlight," said Charlie with a grin. He was over his scare now, and the evening's activities promised to be exciting. Switching on the flashlight, he stuck the handle into the sand near the seawall and stood back awaiting further instructions. The shaft of light shone up through the blackness and tossed eerie shadows across the craggy seawall.

"Now, me fine matey, let's be seeing the skull you've brought for this solemn occasion."

Charlie unwrapped Nanabelle's leotard and extracted his army-surplus gas mask. Then he spread the black cloth in the sand beside the light and gingerly laid the skull on it, beaming with pride.

"Auk! gasped Abel Blacklaw. "If that be a skull, it be the skull of a monster or of a long-snouted pig!"

"It's the best I could do," fumbled Charlie. "The *very* best. You don't realize how hard skulls are to get these days."

The ghost was silent, and Charlie wondered if he should confess that it wasn't really a skull after all. He thought it over for a moment and decided that Abel might not reveal his secrets over anything that he thought was not a real skull. Besides, Charlie didn't know how he would explain what an army-surplus gas mask was to someone who had been dead for over two hundred and fifty years. He hadn't even known what a flashlight was.

Finally Abel spoke. "It'll have to do," he said in a grumpy voice. "I hope you fetched a decent quill."

Charlie proudly held up the sea-gull feather, and his invisible friend grunted in approval. "And what about a scrap of parchment? I'm supposing that you knew enough to bring that along, too."

Charlie gulped. He hadn't even thought about paper. Frantically he began searching through his pockets. There was nothing but a rubber band in his shirt, but the lump he extracted from his back jeans pocket was promising. Whatever it was, it had been through the laundry at least once. Charlie poked at it with the point of the quill until it broke open and revealed itself to be a piece of paper that had been folded several times. The outside was useless, but water had not penetrated the inside, and it was smooth and clean.

"Is this good enough?" Charlie asked.

"Aye, matey. It'll do. Now put them on the black cloth beside yer . . . skull," instructed the ghost. "And kneel yourself down in the sand."

Shivers rippled through Charlie as he obeyed. He knelt and placed the quill and paper beside the skull, adjusting their positions a couple of times until they lined up evenly. Then he took a deep breath, folded his hands across his knees, and waited.

There was no sound except that of the waves slapping against the sand for what seemed like an eternity, and the world outside the circle of light was blotted out by total darkness. Charlie's heart began to thump uncomfortably in his chest. Then Abel Blacklaw spoke again.

"Place your right hand on the skull and swear this oath after me."

Charlie put his hand on the skull and gripped it tightly to stop his fingers from trembling.

"I, Charlie Potter," the ghost began.

"I, Charlie Potter," echoed Charlie.

"Do solemnly swear . . ."

"Do solemnly swear . . ."

". . . an oath of loyalty, secrecy, and brother-hood . . ."

". . . an oath of loyalty, secrecy, and brother-hood . . ."

". . . . on this here skull."

". . . . on this here skull."

"Furthermore, if I break this oath . . ."

"Furthermore, if I break this oath . . ."

"*. . . me gizzard'll be cut out and fed to the sharks!*

Charlie gulped and said haltingly, ". . . my giz-zard . . . will be cut out . . . and fed to . . . the . . . sharks."

"Aye, matey. Ye spoke that like a true free-booter. I'm proud of ye, I am."

Charlie tried to smile, but the corners of his mouth put up a struggle.

"There's but one chore left. And then that oath'll be binding upon ye for the rest of your days."

Charlie didn't like the sound of Abel Blacklaw's words, and he eyed the quill that the ghost had said was for writing in blood, frightfully aware that he was the only one present who possessed any blood.

As if he had read Charlie's mind, Abel said, "You'll only be needing a drop or two. Just a prick of your finger'll give you enough to sign your name, and then it'll be done!"

Charlie grabbed the quill and jabbed it into his thumb before he would lose his nerve. He had come this far. He couldn't let himself chicken out now. A drop of blood ballooned on the end of his thumb. Filling the tip of the quill, he began to write. He squeezed his thumb to get more blood and filled the quill again.

When it was finished, Charlie popped his throbbing thumb into his mouth and sucked on his wound while he stared down at the piece of paper with his name written on it in blood where it lay beside the skull.

From the other side of the black cloth laughter danced on the air. "Put out your torch, matey, and cock your ear," Abel Blacklaw said. "I've a marvelous tale to tell!"

CHAPTER 10

CHARLIE HESITATED a moment and then flicked off the flashlight. The full moon, which had not been visible in the glare of the flashlight, seemed to flash on as if answering some secret coded message. Below, its reflections floated in the waters of the Sound like bits of broken glass.

From the other side of the black cloth Abel Blacklaw grunted softly, as if he were settling into a comfortable position from which to recount his tale. Charlie fidgeted, knowing that the moment he had waited for was nearly at hand. Very shortly the secrets of the ghost of the gravestone hearth would be his, too.

Abel cleared his throat and began speaking in a serious tone. "There was nary a sliver of moon that night, matey. The sky was as black as a parson's hat. It was our seventh night out and my first voyage aboard me father's trading ship, the *Sarah,* out of Portsmouth, New Hampshire. I was anxious to do him proud since I was the oldest of a pack of six boys and the first to go to sea.

"I had snuck up to the deck for a bit of air after all me mates were a-snoring, and just as I was leaning across the starboard railing gulping in the salty air and gazing out to sea, a piece of the darkness seemed to roll itself up, forming itself into a sort of ball. Well, matey, the devil fetch me sure if that ghostly form didn't grow and grow, and as it grew it got closer and closer to the *Sarah*.

"I scrunched myself down as low as I could get and still see over the railing, but on it came, heading straight for us, and getting bigger and bigger as it came.

"Then suddenly the clouds ripped open and moonlight shot out like cannon fire, lighting up the sea and everything on it. When I looked for that gob of blackness I'd seen floating off our starboard, I saw what it really was—a pirate ship! The *Sea Dragon* was the name painted on her bow, and she had bloody cutthroats lining her deck and the Jolly Roger crowning her masts!"

Charlie gasped. "What did you do then?"

"What did I do, matey? Well, I commenced a-bellering like a cow in labor because I could see that they were lowering longboats and getting ready to board us. Let me tell you, they were a mangy-looking lot, enough to scare the devil himself, as they climbed our ropes and sprang onto our decks. There was them with stubs for hands and them with stumps for legs and them with patched-over eyes and blood-red scars. They had knives in their teeth and pistols in their belts and there was hate spitting out of their eyes.

"Our crew was dazed, having mostly been rousted up out of their sleep, but they didn't hang back from the fight. Pistols cracked and swords scraped, and before long the deck was awash with blood. Since I had no weapon, I hung in the shadows watching the fracas until I couldn't stand it any longer. Pirates and sailors alike were falling left and right. Each time a man fell, I made a dash to recover his weapon and make it my own, but another was always quicker. Finally one of those cutthroats fell at my feet, shot through the heart and deader'n a mackerel. His sword was gone and so was his gun, but he still had his boots, so I jerked one off and jumped out of the shadows swinging that dead man's boot over my head like a cutlass.

"I don't mind telling you, I was a sight to see, cracking heads and bashing faces with the heel of that boot. A regular dervish I was, whirling and spinning all over that deck sending freebooters sprawling every which way."

Charlie nodded furiously as visions of young Abel Blacklaw's fearless deeds danced in his head. "Go on! Go on!" he shouted.

The ghost heaved a great sigh. "There's not much more to tell of the fight," he said dejectedly. "I had no sooner gotten into it than it was over. There were many wounded and dead, including me father, Captain Hosmer Blacklaw, and they stripped the rest of us of what weapons we had and locked us in the hold until cockcrow.

"A sorrier sight you couldn't imagine as was I when I crawled into the daylight. I had spent the night in the belly of that ship grieving for me poor dead father and thinking of me poor mother, Sarah Blacklaw, and how I would have to tell the sad news to her. A few of the sailors were praying at the top of their voices, and some were moaning and grunting with painful wounds, and more than a few were cursing the fiendish blacklegs that held us prisoner aboard our own ship. Their booty was piled in the middle of the deck, and they stood around it grinning and toasting each other with good rum from the stores of the *Sarah*.

"The pirate captain was a man named Finn, and I've seen sharks with a kinder look. He stood close to seven feet tall, and the shadow he cast in the low morning sun was near to the length of the ship. Finn spat in the direction of us quivering sailors and plunked a bag of coins onto a table that had been brought out for him. There was a chair there, too, and he folded his big self up and sat down. The pirates that had been injured in the fracas commenced to line up, eyeing the bag of coins.

"The first man had lost his left hand, and the stub was wrapped in a bloody rag. 'Five hundred pieces of eight or five slaves!' bellowed Captain Finn. Those words struck fear into our hearts, for all of us preferred walking the plank to spending our lives as a cutthroat's slave. The pirate gave us all an evil-eyed look, but his greedy nature won him over and he scooped up the coins and was gone.

"There were ten in all to be paid for their wounds, and handsome was the price they got. Five hundred pieces of eight for a left arm, six hundred for a right, five hundred pieces of eight for a right leg, and four hundred for a left. An eye was worth one hundred pieces of eight, and so was a finger, but both eyes lost was worth a thousand. Since a slave from the captured ship could be taken for every hundred pieces of eight, we stood there shaking and trembling while the captain doled out the coins.

"One by one they grabbed their money until there was only one left, and we were breathing easier. 'Twas Skinhead, the bald-headed first mate, and he came up last, snarling and cursing and holding his right eye. He was a horrible sight with dried blood stuck on his face and a greasy red beard that had left an oily streak on the front of his coat. He squinted his good eye and scowled at the coins while Captain Finn counted them out.

" 'Keep your filthy money!' Skinhead roared. 'Give me the slimy devil who put out my eye with the *bloody heel of a boot!*' "

Charlie gasped. "Did he know who had done it? Did he know it was you?"

"Well, matey, you can be sure I was wondering the very same thing as he stomped over to where we sailors crouched in mortal fear and commenced to study us one at a time. I stood there shaking, and under my breath I promised the Lord uncommonly good behavior if I was spared. Out of the corner of an eye I could see him coming down the line, getting closer and closer, with his big belly sticking out like the bow of a ship, I closed my eyes and prayed some more, offering to strike up any kind of bargain. Then sour breath closed over me face like a mask, and I braced meself, knowing in my heart what was going to come next.

" 'So there you are,' growled Skinhead. His scratchy voice was low and sinister, so that besides me only them standing close around could hear. 'Take him away!' he shouted and cuffed me one, and I went sprawling across the deck."

CHAPTER 11

ABEL BLACKLAW paused, and Charlie wondered if remembering was painful for the ghost. Still, it had been Abel's idea to tell the story, and Charlie could hardly wait to hear more.

"What was it like, being a pirate's slave?" he asked. "Was it awful?"

"Aye, awful it was, matey. They drug me aboard the *SEA DRAGON* kicking and screaming for all I was worth, but I might as well have gone easy for all the good it did me. The things that happened the next few weeks are too horrible to tell. There was me bowing and scraping to Skinhead and working until me back was nearly broke, and there was him, fat and lazy, piled up in his bunk gnawing on a bone like the dog that he was, wiping his greasy fingers on his beard and laughing while he ordered me around. I can tell ye sure that hate for that cutthroat was growing inside me like a tumor.

"I had only one friend on that floating pest hole, a scrawny pirate named Baitfish. He got that name from being nipped at by a school of bluefish who mistook him for a fish, and his body was covered with scarred-over holes where they bit him. Ugly as he was,

68

he didn't have many friends among the other pirates, so he'd sneak to see me when nobody was looking and bring me extra portions of food.

"But like I was telling you, old Skinhead worked me pretty nearly to death. There were only a few times when I got to rest. I could always tell when one of those times was coming. First, I'd hear sailors scurrying around on the deck and then shouting that a trading ship had been sighted. Right after that, old Skinhead would go for his rum to build up his courage for the fight. He would commence to drink it as soon as the ship was sighted, even though the *SEA DRAGON* would lay back and wait for the cover of night to attack. Along about dusk Skinhead would grab me by my hair, kick me a couple of times, and push me down into the hold, where I'd stay locked up tight until the trader was taken and the fight was over.

"We cruised the Atlantic Ocean plundering ships until the *SEA DRAGON* nearly burst with so much booty. Mostly it was dry goods and tools bound for the Colonies, but there was one sea chest full of gold that Captain Finn guarded night and day. After what I reckon was about two months, Captain Finn ordered his ship to sail into Long Island Sound, and Baitfish whispered to me that he was looking for a place to bury the gold.

"Late that night while the *SEA DRAGON* lay at anchor, Skinhead ordered me into a longboat. Captain Finn was already in it and so was the chest of gold, and the longboat was lowered and the three of us rowed ashore. It took all three of us to drag the chest up to the spot where it was to be buried. Then Captain

Finn brought out a skull wrapped in black cloth and a quill for writing in blood, and while I looked on, the two of them swore an oath of loyalty, secrecy, and brotherhood."

Shivers climbed up Charlie's back like a parade of ants.

"You mean . . . like the oath I just swore?"

"The very one. There was terror in my heart as they swore it because there I was, just watching instead of swearing with them, and I knew that they meant to kill me as soon as the gold was buried.

"They set me to work digging a hole while they sprawled out to watch and swig down rum. Being a clever lad, I set me a pace for digging that hole that would of taken at least all night. 'Twasn't long until they passed out cold, and then I found me a spot a few yards away, and I dug me a hole of me own."

"And stole the gold away from the pirates?" asked Charlie in disbelief.

"Aye, matey, that's just what I did, and hard work it was, too. That chest was too heavy to budge by meself, so I had to devise a plan for getting it moved."

"What did you do?"

"Well, you heard me say that I was a clever lad, and I took off me shirt and filled it with as many bags of gold as it would hold. Then I drug me booty to the hole I had dug for meself and went back for more. I must of made twenty trips before I got it all and the chest, too, while Captain Finn and Skinhead was laying there sleeping it off. I put the chest down in the hole, pushed the bags of gold in it, and covered it up."

"Wow!" said Charlie. "You really had nerve!"

"Aye, I was as brave as I was clever, 'tis true. But that's not the end of me story. It was nearly dawn by the time I got that chest buried and was busy covering up me tracks when old Skinhead woke up with a roar. He came rising up off the ground swatting flies in his beard and cursing to the top of his lungs, which of course woke up Captain Finn. The two of them was a sight to see, staggering and swearing after me and the gold. But I didn't have time for enjoying the spectacle. I was hidden behind a sand dune no more'n twenty feet from the two of them. The sun was coming up fast, and I knew I had to hurry if I was going to get away.

"The beached longboat seemed to be me best chance, and I turned on me belly and slithered along the valleys of the sand heading toward the water. Behind me, I could hear Captain Finn and old Skinhead thrashing around.

"Everything was going fine until I ran out of low places in the sand. Between me and that longboat was a wide, smooth stretch of beach. 'Twas then I knew I'd made a poor choice of ways to escape, but the choice had been made, and there was nothing to do but make a run for it.

"I had no sooner sprung to me feet than they saw me and came tearing across the sand, Captain Finn tall as a tree and Skinhead puffing along beside him with his greasy beard flopping against his belly. I reached the boat and gave it a shove, but it was heavy and awkward and slow to float, so I left it and splashed on out until I reached deep water. Ahead of me the *Sea Dragon* floated on the waves like a sleeping monster, and behind me Captain Finn and Skinhead were bearing down fast.

"I gulped me some air and dove down under water, which was me second mistake. Me boots were as heavy as lead, and they drug me toward the bottom like a pair of anchors. Me arms and shoulders ached from digging all night, but I gathered together what strength I could and pushed upward. With lungs bustin', I crashed through the surface and bounced against Skinhead's belly. I heard a cry behind me and swirled around just in time to catch Captain Finn's fist in the side of the head. That sent me bouncing off Skinhead's belly again, but this time I grabbed hold of his beard and yanked him face first underwater. Then that rum-soaked old blackleg grabbed me ankles, and as I spun over in the water the toe of me left boot shot up under Captain Finn's chin.

"Well, we was all three too tired to fight very long—them from too much rum and me from too much digging. I was out of air and aching for rest, and the water was cool and soothing, and the bubbles were swirling around me, and I closed me eyes and went to sleep."

"You mean . . . you . . . you drowned?" asked Charlie in disbelief.

"Aye, matey. That's just what I did, but I took those bloody cutthroats with me to the bottom of the sea." There was a note of pride in Abel Blacklaw's voice as he finished his story, and he seemed to settle back for a moment of silent reflection.

Charlie was silent, too, but his head was dizzy with thoughts of Abel Blacklaw's courage and daring and of bloodthirsty pirates and buried gold and of his ghostly friend's wet and slimy death. Suddenly one thought seemed to separate itself from all the rest, and Charlie cast a puzzled look toward the spot in the darkness from which the ghost's voice had come.

"The gold," he whispered. "If you were the only one who knew where it was buried and you drowned, whatever happened to the gold?"

Laughter echoed in the darkness. "Well, matey, I thought you'd never ask. It's still here somewhere along this very stretch of beach, and you and I are going to dig it up!"

At the sound of Abel's words, sirens went off inside Charlie's head, firecrackers exploded in his ears, and a sense of excitement flooded over him that almost took his breath away.

"Pirate gold is buried *here* . . . on this beach?" he whispered.

"For all I know, ye could be sitting on it!" said the ghost. "The shoreline looks a mite different than it did back then. There was nary a house for miles in either direction, but wherever it is, we'll dig it up, we will."

"Don't you have *any* idea where it is?" asked Charlie, looking around the moonlit sand as if expecting a signboard to pop up and point the way. He tried not to think about how long it would take to dig up the entire beach.

"I've been studying about it for the last few days, matey, and I've decided that it's over there, the second private beach down, going toward the public beach."

Charlie groaned. It was one thing to have to dig

up the beach to find the gold, but it was even worse to have to dig on someone else's private property.

"A lot of good it'll do us there," he muttered. "If we try to dig it up, we'll get arrested. Or at least, I will."

"That's why we're going to dig at night. At midnight, to be exact, after everybody in all the houses has gone to sleep. You can sneak out of your room, just like you did tonight, and you can bring some shovels and picks. And don't forget your torch."

Charlie's head was still spinning as he said good night to Abel Blacklaw a little while later and sneaked back to his room. The house was dark and quiet, and he snuggled into his bed sure that no one knew that he had been gone. This was going to be easy, he thought. It might just be the easiest thing he'd ever done, and he turned onto his side and fell asleep dreaming.

CHAPTER 12

MRS. POTTER and Nanabelle never went near the beach during the week, but on weekends, when Mr. Potter was down from Poughkeepsie, the entire family always trooped down to the water's edge to spend the day. Today was no exception, and Charlie helped his mother set up her beach umbrella, wishing that it were any day of the week but Sunday. He wanted desparately to be alone so that he could look around and study the beach and get prepared for his midnight rendezvous with Abel Blacklaw. Maybe he would even draw a map—if no one was watching him, that is.

Charlie need not have worried. Mr. Potter unfolded an aluminum chaise lounge, settled into it, and was snoring in less than three minutes. Nanabelle smeared greasy suntain oil all over her arms and legs and stretched out on a beach towel, and Mrs. Potter quickly absorbed herself in a paperback book that she dug out of her beach bag. Maybe this wasn't going to be so bad after all, thought Charlie.

He swam for a while and poked along the water's edge for shells, but his attention was on the private beach two houses away where Abel Blacklaw had said that the treasure was buried. Charlie tried to imagine what it had been like on that fateful night when young Abel Blacklaw had come ashore with Captain Finn and Skinhead. He could almost see them dragging the heavy chest across the sand and then the two cutthroats sprawling on the ground drinking rum and laughing drunkenly while Skinhead's slave buried the gold.

For a fleeting moment Charlie wondered if the gold was still there. After all, thousands of people had been along this beach in the past two hundred and fifty years. Maybe even millions. And lots of them liked to dig in the sand.

Charlie studied the section of beach where the gold lay hidden for distinguishing characteristics that might be important when he drew his map. For one thing, there was no seawall dividing the yard from the beach. Instead, the lawn sloped down gently to mix with and then become sand. And there was a small jetty pointing out into the water like a finger, which probably had helped Abel Blacklaw recognize the spot. Aside from that, the beach was pretty much like all the others.

Charlie poured himself a glass of lemonade from a thermos his mother had brought along and looked at his watch. It was only eleven fifteen. It wasn't even lunchtime, and he had to wait twelve hours and forty five minutes until it was time to dig for gold. This day was going to last forever.

He finished his lemonade and started sucking on an ice cube, but the cold ice made his teeth ache, so he spit the ice back into his paper cup. He lay back in the warm sand and closed his eyes, trying to imagine what it was going to be like being rich. He'd have a chauffeur-driven limosine all his own, of course, and live in a mansion.

Suddenly his thoughts were punctured by a scream. It was Nanabelle, and Charlie opened his eyes just in time to see her swoop down on him and begin pounding on his chest.

"You little monster!" she shrieked. "You *creepy* little monster!"

"What did I do?" cried Charlie, fending off the blows as best he could.

"This is what you did," she said with a fiendish grin. Then she opened one of her fists and dropped an ice cube onto Charlie's stomach. "And now you know how it feels!"

Charlie came up off the sand with a howl as the knife of cold pierced his body. He lunged for Nanabelle, who was backing away, and caught her by the ankle, sending her sprawling into the sand.

"I didn't do it!" he shouted. "How could I? I was . . . asleep."

"I don't know how you did it, but you *did* it!" said Nanabelle, making a terrible face as she tried to jerk her ankle free of Charlie's grasp.

Just then Mr. Potter appeared, looming above them like a mountain. His hair was tousled and although his eyes were puffy from sleep, anger shone brightly in them. "What's going on here?" he demanded.

"Charlie threw ice on me while I was sunbathing, the creepy little monster." Nanabelle pushed her lower lip out into a pout and looked up at her father with pitiful eyes.

Charlie sighed. There was no use protesting. It

would only make things worse. "Okay. Okay. So you got back at me. Go back to your sun worshiping and let me sleep."

By this time Mrs. Potter had come over to see what the disturbance was. "You're going to have to do something with that boy, Frank," she said, shaking her head sadly. "He picks on poor Nanabelle unmercifully."

"Later, Florence," said Mr. Potter. "We're paying a fortune for this place. Let's try to enjoy it." Then, giving Charlie a stern look, he added, "*If* we can."

Charlie scowled at Nanabelle and flopped over onto his stomach. Abel Blacklaw was at it again. There was just no other explanation. But why did he have to pick on Nanabelle, of all people?

If only his friend Henry were here, he thought. He really missed Henry, and no adventure that they had been able to imagine together had ever been as exciting as meeting a real ghost and digging for pirate treasure.

The day at the beach finally ended, and Mr. Potter announced that he would barbecue chicken on the patio. To Charlie's delight, Nanabelle went slinking off to her room complaining of a sunburn and didn't come down for dinner. He waited until the moment seemed right and then brought up the subject of Henry.

"Dad," he began. "Do you think it would be all right if you brought Henry along next weekend?"

Mr. Potter frowned. "Do you really think you deserve a treat like that? You certainly haven't been behaving very well lately."

Charlie stared glumly into his plate. He had been

afraid that his father might bring that up. Then Mrs. Potter surprised him.

"I don't know, Frank. It might keep him out of trouble if he had someone here to play with."

Charlie listened quietly while his parents discussed the pros and cons of Henry's visit, and after what seemed a terribly long time, they agreed that Henry could come down from Poughkeepsie with Mr. Potter the next Saturday.

Excusing himself, Charlie went to his room as soon as it was dark and set his alarm clock for midnight, just in case he accidentally fell asleep. Then he began writing a letter to Henry, which his father would take with him when he left the beach house the next morning. He promised Henry a great adventure, but he decided to keep the ghost and the buried treasure a secret until Henry got there.

After he finished the letter, he started to draw a treasure map. He marked off the houses and their private beaches and drew the jetty out into the Sound, but he would have to finish it later since he didn't know yet where to put the x.

Charlie heard his parents come up to bed about eleven o'clock. He waited half an hour and then pushed in the alarm button on his clock so that it wouldn't go off at midnight and wake the whole house, and then slipped out of his room. Clicking on his flashlight, he made his way down the dark stairs and into the garage. He couldn't find a pick, but there were two shovels leaning against the back wall of the garage. He picked them up, turned off the flashlight, and made his way onto the moon-drenched lawn.

He hurried down the path to the beach, where

the sand lay as pale as snow in the bright moonlight. Looking back, he saw that his own house was dark, and a quick glance up and down the shore revealed that all the other houses were dark, too.

Although he had plenty of time, Charlie trotted off toward the private beach where Abel Blacklaw had said the gold was buried. The shovels clunked loudly as he dropped them onto the sand, and he stood beside them waiting nervously for his invisible friend.

CHAPTER 13

CHARLIE DID not have long to wait.

"Over here," came a voice out of the darkness.

Charlie picked up the shovels and followed the sound to a spot where tufts of grass dotted the sand. It was almost in the backyard of the house to which the private beach belonged, and besides that, it was less than six feet from a sign that warned, NO TRES-PASSING.

"We can't dig here," insisted Charlie, putting down the shovels carefully so that they did not make any noise. "Even if they don't catch us tonight, they'll be sure to see the hole tomorrow."

"Well, matey, if this be where the gold is buried, there's not much use of digging anywhere else," grumbled the ghost.

Charlie knew that Abel was right. "We'll have to be extra careful, then," he said. "And I don't dare turn on my . . . torch. The moon's making plenty of light, anyway."

Abel Blacklaw grunted in agreement, and one of the shovels rose into the air. Charlie swallowed a giggle as he watched the shovel dig into the ground and raise a scoop of dirt seemingly by itself.

"Are you going to help me dig, or would you rather stretch out in the sand with a bottle of rum and watch?" Abel asked impatiently.

"Sorry," said Charlie. "It's just that I never saw a shovel dig a hole all by itself before."

"All by itself!" shouted the ghost.

"Shhhh!" warned Charlie. "You're going to wake somebody."

The digging was easy in the soft, sandy soil, and neither of them spoke as they worked. Soon the *shish-whook, shish-whook* sound made by the shovels and dirt fell into time with the gentle lapping of waves against the shore.

The hole grew deeper and deeper, and Charlie wondered silently how much longer they would have to dig. Abel must have wondered the same thing because every so often his shovel would stop its digging, as if the ghost were pausing to think.

The night was warm, and Charlie stripped off his shirt, wishing that he had thought to bring along something to drink. Beside him, Abel Blacklaw's shovel stopped again.

"The devil fetch me, matey, but I think we're digging in the wrong spot."

"What?" cried Charlie. "What do you mean, we're digging in the wrong spot? You were the one who picked it in the first place."

"Aye, right ye are, and I can only beg your forgiveness for such a terrible transgression."

Charlie sighed. In spite of all his mischief, it was just about impossible to be angry with Abel Blacklaw. "Okay," he said, smiling at his invisible friend in the darkness. "But we'd better fill up this hole before we start digging a new one."

Within a few minutes the hole had been refilled and the dirt patted smooth on the top.

"Now where?" asked Charlie. His arms and shoulders were beginning to ache and his back was tired from so much stooping over, but the thought of all that gold waiting beneath their feet renewed Charlie's energy and made him want to dig some more.

The ghost was silent for a moment, and Charlie thought he heard Abel mumbling to himself. "I'll just go down to the water's edge for a wider view," he said a moment later.

Abel was gone for several minutes, but when he returned his spirits were high. "I've got it right this time, matey. You can bile me in oil, if I haven't. I was just a smidgen off in me calculations the first time."

Abel Blacklaw's shovel raised to a slant and appeared to drag itself farther into the yard. Charlie picked up his own shovel and followed cautiously. There was no use to object. But he wished with all his might that they weren't moving closer to the house.

"This is it," said the ghost. At that same instant, his shovel raised into the air and dropped, sticking upright in the dirt like a signpost.

Charlie squared his shoulders and began to dig. The sooner they got this over, the better. If they could just get the gold and get out of there, they would be all right. But how were they going to get a heavy chest up out of the ground once they found it? And where would they hide it when they did?

Charlie leaned wearily on his shovel. He was just

about to open his mouth and ask Abel when he heard a sound at the house. Suddenly the back-porch light flashed on, spilling yellow light in a wide circle across the yard. A man wearing only baggy undershorts stepped out the door, followed by an enormous black dog. The man yawned loudly and stretched his arms up over his head.

"Okay, Rasputin, old boy. Just don't stay out here too long." The man turned and went back into the house, but Rasputin trotted down the porch steps and into the backyard.

Charlie held his breath, trying not to move so much as an eyelash. Abel Blacklaw's shovel was motionless, too. If Rasputin saw them, they were doomed. The huge dog looked like a Labrador retriever, and the shadow he cast in the porch light was the size of a dinosaur. As big as he was, his bark could probably bring out the entire beach-front population, and if he decided to go after them, he could more than likely gobble them up like pork-chop bones. Then Charlie remembered that Rasputin couldn't see Abel, and his heart pounded harder than ever.

Rasputin sniffed urgently at the ground. He trotted in circles, sniffing a twig here or a blade of grass there and picking up speed as he went. Charlie exhaled slowly and began to fill his lungs again. Maybe Rasputin would take care of his business and go back into the house without ever knowing that Charlie was there. It was almost too much to hope for.

Rasputin zigzagged around the yard and disappeared behind a tree.

"Maybe I should make a run for it," Charlie whispered in the direction of the upright shovel.

The shovel hit the ground with a thunk.

"Don't leave me here with that monster dog," whispered Abel. His voice was filled with panic. "I'm begging you, matey. Please don't leave me with'im."

Charlie couldn't believe his ears. Abel Blacklaw was afraid of dogs.

"But you're invisible," argued Charlie. "He won't even know you're here."

"He'll know, all right. You can take me word for that."

At that moment Rasputin came from behind the tree. He was still hurrying along, his legs churning and his nose bouncing along the ground. Suddenly he stopped, pricked up his ears, and looked toward the spot where Charlie and Abel stood. Softly, almost inaudible at first, he began to growl.

"See! What did I tell ye?" Abel whispered hoarsely.

Charlie tightened the grip on his shovel. He didn't want to hurt the animal, but he didn't want to be eaten alive, either. He almost wished that the man in baggy undershorts would come out again, even though it was sure to mean trouble.

Rasputin seemed to have forgotten all about the business that had been so urgent a moment before. Slowly, one paw at a time, he crept toward Charlie and his invisible friend.

"You've got to do something," begged Abel. "You've got to lead him away from me or something."

"Sure," said Charlie. "And let him turn me into a ghost, too? You've got to be kidding!"

On came Rasputin, and the closer he came, the louder he growled. Charlie swallowed hard and tried to remember everything he had ever been told about unfriendly dogs. Stay calm. Don't make any sudden moves. Don't let the dog know that you're afraid.

"Nice doggy. Nice Rasputin. That's a good boy," said Charlie in a small, quivery voice.

Rasputin stopped where he was and looked at Charlie, and Charlie had the odd feeling that the dog had not noticed him before. Rasputin had stopped growling and was wagging his tail.

"See. What did I tell ye, matey. He knows I'm here, all right. Dogs has got a special sense when it comes to ghosts."

At the sound of Abel's hoarse whisper, Rasputin shifted his gaze toward the ghost's fallen shovel and began to growl again. This time his upper lip curled back, showing needle-sharp fangs.

"It's okay, boy. It's okay," called Charlie. He extended his hand and took a step toward Rasputin, who sniffed at it, one finger at a time, before wagging his tail in approval of their friendship. Charlie knelt and stroked the dog's head, paying special attention to the spot behind each ear where he knew most dogs like to be scratched. Rasputin closed his eyes and leaned against Charlie. He seemed to be lost in rapture.

Charlie whispered to Abel out of the corner of his mouth, "Now's your chance. Slip away and meet me on our beach. I'll come along and bring the shovels as soon as I can."

There was no reply from the ghost, and Charlie continued to pet Rasputin, trying to allow plenty of time for Abel to get away.

Suddenly the back door of the house opened and

the man in baggy undershorts came out again. This time he didn't seem the least bit sleepy as he stomped down the steps and into the yard.

Charlie's heart sank like an anchor as the man began scanning the yard and calling, "Where are you, boy? You've been out here long enough. Here, Rasputin. Here, boy."

CHAPTER 14

A SHIVER raced up Charlie's backbone as he surveyed all the evidence of his guilt. A hole in the backyard of a house where a NO TRESSPASSING sign was prominently displayed. Two shovels. One boy. Of course he could simply explain that the ghost of Abel Blacklaw had said that there was a chest of pirates' gold buried in that spot and that the two of them had met at midnight to dig it up. But who would believe a story like that even though it was true?

So far, the man in baggy undershorts had not seen Charlie, so he nudged Rasputin and whispered, "Go on, boy. Go to your master."

Rasputin gazed up at Charlie and then licked him tenderly on the hand, as if he were content to stay there for the rest of the night.

Charlie nudged Rasputin a little harder. "Go on," he insisted. Any instant the man in baggy undershorts would spot him and it would be all over.

"Come on, Rasputin. You've been out there long enough," the man called impatiently.

Suddenly Rasputin seemed to remember the urgent business that had brought him outside in the first place, and he loped off in the direction of his master, sniffing the ground as he went.

Charlie scrunched down, trying to make himself as small as possible, and closed his eyes. Maybe the man in baggy undershorts would think he was a rock or a bush or something like that if he saw him. Maybe he wouldn't notice Charlie at all. He sat very still until he heard the sound of the back door closing, and just as he opened his eyes the light flicked off. Charlie heaved a sigh of relief. They had gone inside.

Charlie did not move for a few minutes, until he felt sure that both man and dog were settled for the night. Then he slipped on his shirt, loosely replaced the dirt in the hole, and picked up the shovels. Maybe the man in baggy undershorts wouldn't even notice that someone had been digging in his yard, thought Charlie as he trudged wearily across the private beaches toward his own. Maybe they could try again tomorrow night.

Following Charlie's instructions, the ghost was waiting beside the seawall.

"Many thanks to ye, matey," said Abel. "I've just about recovered from me fright."

"Well, how are we going to dig up the gold if you're scared of Rasputin?" grumbled Charlie.

"Aye, matey. We'll dig it up, all right. Tomorrow night we'll bring along something to distract that monster dog."

"Like what?" asked Charlie gruffly. He was tired, and what was more, he resented Abel's calling Rasputin a monster dog.

"A beefsteak, matey. A beefsteak!" chirped the ghost. "Show me a dog that can't be distracted by a beefsteak, and I'll show you a dead dog."

"A *steak!* You've got to be kidding. Where in the world are we going to get a steak?"

"You're going to get it from your mother's kitchen. Surely in such a fine house as that, there's at least one teensy-weensy beefsteak."

Charlie swallowed hard. He couldn't go stealing a steak.

"Think of the gold," said Abel, as if he had read Charlie's mind. "Isn't all that gold worth stealing one teensy-weensy beefsteak for?"

Charlie didn't answer. Abel had a point. Even if his parents found out about the steak, they wouldn't be able to be angry once they saw the trunkful of gold.

Yawning deeply, Charlie agreed to bring a steak with him when they met at midnight the following night. Then he lifted the shovels under one arm and headed for home and his bed.

The next morning Charlie barely made it down to breakfast before his father left for Poughkeepsie. He decided not to wash his face or comb his hair, since it hurt to raise his arms, and he slipped into a pair of shorts and a T shirt, grabbed his letter to Henry, and trudged down the stairs.

"Well, if it isn't death warmed over," remarked Nanabelle when Charlie entered the kitchen. "You look like you've been up all night."

Charlie started to make a nasty crack about Nanabelle's sunburn, but his head was throbbing and his eyes burned, and he didn't feel up to an argument, so he just ignored her.

"You do look a little pale," said Mrs. Potter, feeling his forehead and cheeks for signs of fever. "I hope you're not coming down with something."

"Naw," said Charlie. "I just didn't sleep very

well. There was a mosquito in my room. It kept buzz-
ing in my ear all night."

Mrs. Potter seemed satisfied and turned back to
frying pancakes. Mr. Potter drained his coffee cup and
looked at his watch. "I'd better get going," he said
with a sigh. "The traffic is going to be murder out
there this morning."

He gave Mrs. Potter and Nanabelle each a light
kiss on the cheek and then put a hand on Charlie's
shoulder. "I expect to get a better report on you this
week, son," he said sternly. "After all, you're the man
of the house while I'm gone. I'd like for you to behave
that way."

"Yes, sir," Charlie answered dutifully. "And,
Dad . . . here's a letter to Henry inviting him to come
down with you next weekend."

Mr. Potter took the letter, gave Charlie a friendly
pat on the back, and was gone. Mrs. Potter set a plate
of pancakes in front of Charlie and sat down to her
own breakfast. The room was silent as the three of
them concentrated on their food. Charlie eyed the refrigerator while he ate, wondering what the chances
were that there would be a steak inside. If they had
steak for dinner, it was usually on the weekend, when
Mr. Potter was there. This was only Monday. With a
sigh, Charlie finished his breakfast and excused himself.

Back in his room, he sprawled across the bed. A
night of digging for treasure had left him exhausted,
and the softness of the bed was welcome. Soon he
drifted off to sleep. It was a long time later when he
awoke, and he could not be sure what had awakened

him. The sun had climbed high into the sky, and sunlight was streaming in the window, making his room hot and stuffy.

He sat up stiffly and looked around. Something was wrong. He could feel it, but he didn't know what it was. Nanabelle's probably nosing around, trying to spy on me, he thought, but a quick glance toward the door revealed that it was firmly latched.

Deciding that his imagination was playing tricks on him, he went to the window and opened it, breathing deeply the refreshing cool air. By pushing the side of his face against the screen, he could just barely see the beach and backyard two houses away, where he and Abel Blacklaw had dug for gold. There was no sign of the man in baggy undershorts or of Rasputin, and he couldn't be sure if the brownish-colored spot near the center of the yard was the hole that he and Abel had made or not.

Charlie shuddered. For some reason the whole thing seemed a lot scarier in the daylight than it had at night. Maybe it was because he had felt hidden by the darkness, he mused.

Suddenly there was a loud rap somewhere behind him. Charlie whirled around. His heart was pounding as he surveyed the room. It was hard to tell if anything had been disturbed, since neatness was not one of Charlie's major traits, but everything seemed in place. It was probably someone at the door, he thought. Charlie opened the door a crack and peered out, but no one was there. Closing the door, he faced the gravestone.

"Abel," he called softly, "is that you?"
There was no reply.

CHAPTER 15

"ABEL BLACKLAW, I know you're in here," said Charlie. "Now quit horsing around and say something."

Still, there was no response from the ghost.

"Okay. Have it your way," Charlie said in a peevish tone. "See if I care."

With that, Charlie sauntered out of his room, slamming the door behind him. Sometimes he got a little irritated at that ghost. So what if he knew where buried pirate gold was? That didn't give him the right to pull tricks on Nanabelle that got Charlie in trouble or to order people to steal steaks or to try to scare somebody half to death. It would serve him right if Charlie didn't show up at all for their rendezvous, much less with a steak for Rasputin.

While he had been thinking all of this, Charlie had absentmindedly wandered to the kitchen and now he found himself standing in front of the refrigerator. His mother was nowhere around, so Charlie opened the refrigerator door and looked inside. He could see right away that there wasn't even one teensy-weensy beefsteak, as Abel had put it. What there was was a roast about the size of his thigh and a chunk of salami.

Charlie eyed the roast. He could never steal a

thing like that and get away with it. Besides, his mother was probably planning to cook it for supper. There was nothing to do but hope that Rasputin liked salami, and Charlie took it out, wrapped it in a piece of plastic wrap, and stuffed it inside his shirt. Now all that was left to do was wait.

He arrived early at the spot where the treasure was buried. He had been hoping that Rasputin would be outside and that there would be a few minutes to play with him before Abel got there and he had to be distracted, but the dog was nowhere in sight. The house was dark, and all was peaceful as Charlie sat down on the grass to listen to the waves brush the shore and wait for Abel Blacklaw.

Once he thought he heard the ghost approaching, but when he called out, there was no reply. Charlie stretched out on his back and studied the stars. There were millions, maybe even billions of them visible tonight.

He lay there for what seemed like a long time, dozing every now and then and reawakening to the brilliance of the canopy of stars above him. Suddenly the peace was broken by the sound of voices. Low voices, like people whispering, but voices just the same. Charlie felt himself stiffen, and he hardly dared to breathe. Someone was coming.

Maybe it was the man in baggy undershorts or, worse yet, maybe it was some kind of beach patrol. How could he explain what he was doing there in the middle of the night with two shovels? If only Abel would come. Since he was invisible, surely he could scare them away.

Charlie listened again, but the whispering had stopped. Maybe whoever they were had moved away, or maybe it was a couple of lovers and they had stopped talking in order to smooch. The last idea made Charlie chuckle and he relaxed a little and sat up. There was no one close by, and when he finally got the courage to look up and down the beach, he could not see anyone there either. It was probably my imagination, he thought.

Just then the voice of Abel Blacklaw boomed out in the darkness: "Well, matey. I'm glad to see you're so prompt, but why haven't ye commenced to dig?"

Charlie ignored the question. He was glad his invisible friend had finally arrived, and was more relieved than he would ever have admitted.

"Did you . . . did you see anyone?" he asked.

"Not a livin', breathin' soul, me lad. We've got a perfect night for digging up pirates' gold."

Charlie shrugged, credited his imagination again, and stood up with shovel in hand. "Then we'd better get at it," he said.

Abel Blacklaw's shovel tilted upward and began scooping up the sandy soil. Charlie watched in fascination for a few seconds, but then, fearing another scolding from the ghost, he began to dig, too.

"Did you remember to bring a bit of a distraction for that monster dog?" Abel asked after they had been digging awhile.

"Yup," said Charlie. He was glad that Abel had not asked if it was a beefsteak. The ghost seemed satisfied, and the two of them dug in silence for a time.

The hole, which measured about three feet across,

had gotten deeper and deeper until finally Charlie jumped inside and began tossing shovelfuls of dirt out over his shoulder. Surely they were getting close to the gold now, he thought excitedly. Any minute one of them would strike the lid of the chest with his shovel.

Charlie strained to put every ounce of strength he had behind his shovel, digging faster and faster, but gradually he noticed that while he had speeded up his own digging, Abel Blacklaw was slowing down. He's probably just getting tired, thought Charlie, but deep down he began to wonder if there might be another reason.

"Abel, are you sure that we've got the right spot this time?" he asked cautiously.

"Of course we've got the right spot," grumbled the ghost. "Just keep your back into your digging and your weather eye peeled for that monster dog."

"Rasputin's not a monster dog," argued Charlie. "He's gentle and friendly. He's just big, that's all. Why, it makes just about as much sense to be afraid of Rasputin as to be afraid of a sea gull."

"Be mighty careful what you say about sea gulls, lad," said Abel in a voice that sent chills up Charlie's back. "And twice as careful not to harm one."

Charlie shuddered, remembering the sea gull that he had seen on the beach a few days before. Did Abel Blacklaw have something to do with that gull? After all, that bird had been the first in a chain of events that had led straight to the ghost of Abel Black-law and buried treasure.

"What's so special about sea gulls?" said Charlie, not wanting to ask but knowing that he needed to know the answer.

"Sea gulls?" said Abel in a whimsical voice. "Why, don'tcha know, Matey, sea gulls are the souls of sailors lost at sea. There's no sailor that's yet been born who would harm the smallest feather on a sea gull."

Charlie stopped digging and leaned dizzily on his shovel. In his mind, he saw the great flocks of sea gulls that populated the beaches and rode the tide swells. They had always seemed so ordinary. But what if each one of them had once been a sailor? Right there on his very own beach there might be birds who had been Vikings and pirates and Americans lost at Pearl Harbor. And there could be whaling captains and slave runners and pleasure-boat sailors who had gone down in the Bermuda Triangle. There could be natives of the South Seas islands and Eskimo fishermen and . . .

"Listen, matey," said Abel. His words cut sharply into Charlie's thoughts.

"Huh?" said Charlie. He listened as hard as he could, but there was no sound except the beating of waves against the shore. Still, he had heard something earlier. Perhaps it hadn't been his imagination after all.

"It's them!" the ghost whispered hoarsely.

"It's *who?*" Fearfully Charlie looked around, but there was no one to be seen, not even Rasputin.

"Hush yourself and fill in this hole. We haven't much time. When it's done, take the shovels and go back to your home. I'll come to ye by and by if I can."

Charlie obeyed without a word. Furiously he shoveled dirt into the hole, and beside him, the ghost worked rapidly, too. Every now and then Charlie stopped for an instant and looked around the deserted beach. Who could it be, he wondered, and what could they want? Inside his chest his heart beat like a loose shutter in a windstorm.

Finally the hole was filled. Charlie picked up the shovels, and without so much as a backward glance he raced toward home, with the salami bouncing inside his shirt.

CHAPTER 16

THE BEACH house was as dark as the inside of a casket as Charlie crept up the creaky old stairs toward his room. He had put away the shovels and had slipped in through the door from the garage, and he did not dare turn on his flashlight for fear of waking his mother or Nanabelle, so he felt along the walls for his door. He was panting from running, and his heart still pounded both from fear and exhaustion.

It was impossible to make any sense out of the situation. He had no idea who had been on the beach, but he was sure that whoever it was had been spying on them while they dug for the gold. Abel Blacklaw had seemed to know who they were. But then he was a ghost and invisible and could float all over the place whenever he wanted to and find things out. Maybe the boys from the volleyball game had discovered that Charlie went alone to the beach at night and had planned to jump him and beat him up. It could be anything like that, and Abel would be likely to know about it. Probably it was just people out for a late stroll along the beach, and Abel didn't want them to stumble onto the gold. Still, there was one thing that worried him. The ghost had said that he would come to Charlie by and by *if he could*. That had to mean that there was danger.

Charlie found the doorknob and turned it with a grateful sigh. He had made it back to the safety of his room, and his body ached for the comfort of his bed.

Once inside, he felt for the light switch and flipped it on, only to stand frozen in horror at what he saw. His room was a wreck. All of his bureau drawers had been dumped upside down onto the floor, and there was scarcely any place to walk among the piles of socks, underwear, and shirts. His bookshelves had been emptied, the top of his desk swept clean, and all of the clothes had been pulled out of his closet and strewn across his bed.

Charlie stifled a cry. Nanabelle was pretty mean, but she would never do a thing like this. Nanabelle! His mother! Were they all right? Obviously someone had broken into the house. The first thing that he had to do was to make sure that his mother and sister were okay, so gingerly he tiptoed out into the hall. He felt his way along the dark corridor until he found the bathroom. It was directly across from Nanabelle's room, and its light would be just enough to allow him to see into her room.

The light flashed on, and Charlie took a deep breath. He was almost afraid to look, but slowly he turned his head and peered cautiously toward his sister's open door. Everything appeared to be all right from where he stood in the bathroom, so he tiptoed across the hallway for a closer look. Charlie sighed. Nothing had been disturbed, and he could hear Nanabelle gurgling contentedly in her sleep.

Charlie's relief was not complete, however. If just *his* room had been ransacked, it could mean only one thing. Whoever had done it had been looking for something there, or, worse yet, for Charlie himself.

Turning off the bathroom light, Charlie hurried back to his own room. He was certain that the intruders were gone, but maybe they had left a clue. His things were in an unbelievable jumble. He would have to get it all cleaned up before his mother saw it and threw a fit. The first thing to do was to clear the bed, and he threw his clothes back into the closet and closed the door so that they would be out of sight. He could always hang them up tomorrow.

Charlie was dizzy from exhaustion, but he knew that he could never sleep until he found some clue that would tell him who had been in his room and what they wanted. He shoved the fallen books into a corner where they would be less noticeable and began scooping up Monopoly money that lay around the floor like fallen leaves. He would shove the money under his bed and sort it out later, he decided, thinking that straightening up his room was not turning out to be such a bad job after all.

He lifted the end of the bedspread and started to push the money under the bed when something under there caught his eye. It was a piece of drawing paper, and as he pulled it out, he saw that it was the treasure map that he had started making the night he wrote the letter to Henry. He had abandoned the map when it was only half finished, and it had probably fallen off his desk and drifted under the bed. Could this be what the intruders had been looking for? If so, it would help explain the voices on the beach. That was almost certain to be the answer. Someone else knew about the treasure and was trying to get to it ahead of Abel and himself. But who?

Charlie shuddered, remembering two mornings before, when he had heard strange sounds in his room and thought that it was Abel Blacklaw playing tricks on him. Could someone have been hiding there and watching him even then?

Folding the map as small as possible, he buried it under the pile of clothing in the closet, put the chunk of salami on his nightstand, and fell into bed. His brain was too numb to think about the intruders any longer. Besides, since they hadn't found the map in his room, it seemed doubtful that they would come back.

The ghost did not make contact with him the next day or all the next night, although Charlie spent most of the time in his room near the gravestone fireplace. Had something happened to him? Where had he gone? Surely something was wrong.

Thursday came, and still there was no sign of Abel, and Charlie went to bed that night filled with panic. But when he awoke Friday morning, his panic had been replaced by determination. He sat up in his bed with a smile on his face. He would find the gold himself. There was no way that he could locate his invisible friend or even find out where he had gone, but sitting around doing nothing would only make it easy for the others, whoever they were, to get to the gold first. He couldn't let that happen.

Once he had made that decision, Charlie was faced with another problem. How could *he* find it?

He lay back in bed for a while, pondering the question. Since they had dug so deep without finding anything, he had a feeling that the second spot was not the right one, either. But how could he hope to find it without Abel Blacklaw's help?

Charlie moped around the house most of the morning, trying to think of a way out of his dilemma. After lunch he went down to the beach and spent a long time pitching broken shells into the waves. Every so often he would gaze toward the place where they had dug. What if it wasn't there after all? What if it was another fifty yards away? Abel Blacklaw had buried it over two hundred and fifty years ago. It would be easy for him to make that kind of mistake. If only there was some way to see under the ground.

See under the ground? That was it! Suddenly Charlie knew what he had to do. He had to find a way to borrow the metal detector from Fixin' John. The gold was metal, and the chest itself was bound to have a metal lock, so if he swept the beach and dug every time the detector signaled metal, he was certain to find the gold. Charlie let out a joyous whoop and headed for the public beach at a run.

CHAPTER 17

THE CROWD at the public beach had already begun to thin as mothers were gathering their little ones in and heading for home to begin preparing the evening meal. This was the time of day that Fixin' John began sweeping over the sand with his metal detector searching for money, jewelry, and other valuables lost by the day's sunbathers. Charlie looked quickly up and down the long stretch of beach, but Fixin' John and the long-handled detector were nowhere to be seen.

I'm probably early, he thought, and scuffed dejectedly toward the water. A few sea gulls waded near the edge, and Charlie thought briefly about what Abel Blacklaw had said about seagulls being the souls of sailors lost at sea, but he drew his thoughts back quickly to more important problems at hand. It was getting late. Surely Fixin' John would be along any minute. But what then? How could Charlie ever persuade him to lend something as valuable as his metal detector to a boy he barely knew? He sighed and rammed his fists into the pockets of his jeans. He would think of something. He had to.

As it grew later, the beach became more and more deserted, but still there was no sign of Fixin'

John. Maybe he's sick, thought Charlie. Or maybe he's busy in his shop fixing something for somebody. The last thought revived Charlie's spirits. It was a real possibility. After all, fixing was his business, and so surely he had a shop. Probably it was in his house. Charlie guessed that Fixin' John lived somewhere along the beach, since he came every afternoon to sweep the sand. If he could just find his house, there might still be a chance to borrow the metal detector, especially if Fixin' John was too busy to use it himself.

Charlie left the beach and set out along the road at a trot. Most of the houses were summer rentals like his own, but a few were occupied all year round, and they had the names of their owners on the mailboxes that stood beside the road. He read them as he jogged along. Shay. Peebles. Wolfe. Charlie ducked his head as he passed his own house, hoping that no one inside would see him and ask a lot of questions when he got home. Drummond. Casper. Bobatoon. That was it! Fixin' John had said that his name was John Bobatoon.

Charlie stopped and looked at the house. It was an ordinary wooden house, weathered gray, with a white picket fence around the front yard and a rolling, sandy beach behind. No one was in sight.

As he stood there wondering if he should ring the front-door bell, his attention was drawn to a small building at the side of the house that looked as if it might once have been a garage. Now the wide door through which a car could drive had been removed and then filled in with a wall whose boards had not yet weathered to the same shade of gray as the rest of the building, and into that wall an ordinary, people-size door had been inserted. Above this door hung a sign.

FIXIN' JOHN BOBATOON
"If it can be broken,
I can fix it."
ENTRANCE

Charlie picked up a stick and clacked it across the pickets. He knew that he should simply walk up to the door to Fixin' John's shop and knock, but his legs refused to move. The old problem of what to say, how to ask to borrow the metal detector still haunted him, and he was no closer to a solution than he had been before.

There was a window at the side of the shop, and Charlie approached it on tiptoes. He didn't like to sneak, especially when his business was perfectly legal and on the up and up, but perhaps if he could get a peek inside, it would help him decide what course of action he should take next. Blowing sand had left a dusty film across the outside of the pane, and lacy cobwebs clung to the inside corners, but in spite of this Charlie could see the workshop with perfect clarity.

The pegboard walls were hung with every sort of tool, with screwdrivers and chisels, ratchets and saw blades, wrenches and hammers, and underneath the tools were tall bins, similar to the kind in grocery stores that were filled with fruits and vegetables. In the bins were box after box of nails of every size, and screws and washers and pipe connections, and odds and ends that Charlie couldn't identify. An enormous table saw filled one corner, and next to it were numerous other power tools whose uses Charlie couldn't begin to guess. In the center of the room, with his back to Charlie, sat Fixin' John on what looked like a rickety kitchen chair. He was tinkering with something on a bench in front of him, but Charlie couldn't see what it was.

There was a certain amount of order about the shop, although it would never win a Good-House-keeping award, and his own mother would probably faint at the mere sight of such a place. Still, Charlie felt that every object, from the largest saw to the smallest screw, had been placed with respect for its function. Surely Fixin' John was a man with heart.

Charlie marched resolutely to the door while his courage was at its peak. He rapped sharply, knowing that it was now or never.

"Come in. It's open," called Fixin' John from inside.

Without a moment's hesitation Charlie pushed open the door and strode inside. "Hi," he said, pulling the corners of his mouth up into a friendly smile.

"Well, look who's here. If it isn't my friend Charlie from the beach." The tall, lank man looked genuinely pleased, and wrinkles formed around his eyes as he returned the smile. "I suppose you've come about the metal detector?"

"That's right," said Charlie. "I looked for you at the beach, but when you weren't there, I decided . . ."

The words trailed off to a whisper as Charlie noticed for the first time what it was that Fixin' John had been working on when he came in. It was the metal detector, and pieces and parts of it were scattered all over the top of the bench. Charlie stared, not wanting to believe what he saw, and he felt as if his chest were caving in around his heart.

"I suppose you were hoping to try it out again, eh?"

Charlie nodded. He was afraid to try to speak around the lump in his throat. All was lost now. There was no way that he could find the pirates' gold on his own.

Fixin' John chuckled. "Now I thought that I explained to you about believing," he said with mock impatience.

"Yes, sir," murmured Charlie. A lot of good believing would do now. Oh, sure, he believed that Fixin' John could make the metal detector work again, but when? Charlie needed it now.

"You know," said Fixin' John in a faraway voice. "There's believing and then there's *believing*. Most folks believe a little here and a little there, but hardly anyone these days believes with his heart and soul, and that's where the power is."

Charlie's eyes roved to the broken metal detector, his disappointment of a moment ago disolving under a fresh wave of hope. Was it possible that it would really do any good to believe? Could Fixin' John repair it in time?

The handyman must have seen the change in Charlie's mood because he said, "Why, with both of us believing, I'll have this fixed in no time."

Charlie was almost giddy with relief. "Do you think so?" he asked through an enormous grin. Then, remembering the role he was supposed to play, he added, "Of course you will. I *believe*."

Fixin' John gave Charlie the sort of wink that meant they shared a secret, and he began working on the metal detector once more. Charlie watched closely as he fit pieces together and fiddled with wires and tightened screws, concentrating as hard as he could on believing. Fixin' John had said that there was power in believing with your heart and soul, and after a while Charlie could feel tingles and prickles dancing through his body and over his scalp, and squiggles and swirls yo-yoing up and down his spine. It was the power, just like Fixin' John had said. Charlie thought he was going to burst with excitement. Finally he couldn't stand it any longer.

"Do you believe in ghosts?" he blurted.

"Of course," said Fixin' John, without looking up from his work. "Do you?"

That was all the encouragement Charlie needed, and for the next half hour he poured out the story of Abel Blacklaw and the search for buried gold.

Fixin' John smiled and nodded every now and then while Charlie recounted the story. When he had finished, the handyman looked up and said, "I'd heard stories about gold being buried somewhere around here. My, oh, my, what a find that's going to be. Of course, I'll help you, son."

"But the metal detector—will it be working by *midnight?*

"That all depends," said Fixin' John, and Charlie searched the man's face with questioning eyes. "Depends on how much you and I believe."

Charlie promised to believe with all his might,

and the two agreed to meet on the beach at midnight. Charlie tried not to think about how angry Abel would be when he found out that Fixin' John had been let into their secret.

At eleven thirty Charlie slipped out of his room, picked up the shovels in the garage, and headed for the beach. At the last minute he had remembered the salami, which had been out of the refrigerator for more than a day and smelled like a mixture of garlic and old sneakers, but he stuffed it in his shirt just the same.

He had no sooner reached the spot where he and Abel had been digging when a familiar voice rang out in the darkness.

"Well, matey. I'm glad to see your back for another go at it."

CHAPTER 18

JUST AS Charlie had anticipated, when Abel Black-law learned that Fixin' John was going to join their digging party, he blew his invisible top.

"What! You mean to tell me that you've broken your oath? You swore on the skull, remember? You swore loyalty, secrecy, and brotherhood. I've half a mind to feed you to the sharks."

Charlie had forgotten about the oath, and he shivered at the thought of being fed to the sharks. Still, he had only brought Fixin' John into the scheme as a last resort. Abel could certainly be unreasonable sometimes.

"Where have you been, anyway?" he asked, hoping that changing the subject would keep the ghost from carrying out his threat. "Did you find out who was spying on us the other night?"

"I've been spying back, but don't ask who they are," grumbled the ghost. "It's better that you don't know. And stop waggling your jaw and get to digging before you find out firsthand."

What rotten luck, thought Charlie. I get myself a real ghost, and he turns out to be a first-class grouch.

"So how do we know where to dig until Fixin'

John gets here with the metal detector?" Charlie grumbled back at his invisible companion. "It's a cinch *you* don't know where the gold is buried."

As if on cue, Fixin' John appeared before Abel could manage a rebuttal, and to Charlie's great relief, he was carrying the metal detector.

"It worked, Charlie my boy," he said with a wide grin. "All your believing worked, just like I told you it would. Why, I got it fixed with twenty whole minutes to spare."

"Great," said Charlie, feeling a tinge of pride. "Now I'd like for you to meet Abel Blacklaw." It felt a little awkward introducing someone who was invisible, and Charlie gestured in the direction from which the ghost's voice had come, hoping he was still there.

"How do you do, sir," said Fixin' John. "I've heard marvelous things about you from our friend Charlie, and I'm glad to be able to help."

There was no reply, and Charlie thought with growing irritation that Abel Blacklaw was probably pouting. "Abel, say something. It isn't polite not to answer."

Still the ghost was silent.

"Abel!" called Charlie angrily. If he didn't answer soon, Fixin' John might think the whole thing was a hoax and that Charlie had lured him to the beach at midnight on a wild-goose chase.

"It's all right, lad," said Fixin' John. "It's you he trusts. And maybe if we locate his chest of gold, he'll trust me, too."

With that, Fixin' John clamped the earphones on his head, flipped the switch on the metal detector, and began sweeping the moonlit lawn. With a sigh of resignation, Charlie picked up the shovels and followed.

They tramped along in silence for what seemed like ages, moving closer and closer to the water's edge and, to Charlie's great relief, farther and farther from the row of houses. He had assumed the job of lookout, and, sometimes walking backward, he scanned the shoreline for any sign that they were being followed. So far, all was peaceful. Not even Rasputin had shown up, although the chunk of foul-smelling salami was tucked inside Charlie's shirt.

As they walked along, he began complaining to himself about Abel Blacklaw again. That ghost simply had no sense of gratitude. It was Charlie who took all the risks, sneaking shovels out of the garage and salami out of the refrigerator, not to mention himself out of the house at midnight to creep down to a lonely beach where all sorts of grisly things too horrible to imagine might occur. And how did the ghost repay him? By making him look foolish in front of Fixin' John.

Charlie was walking backward while he was thinking all this, but suddenly he came to a stop. He had backed into Fixin' John, and the handyman's face held a look of great concentration.

Charlie excused himself, feeling more foolish than ever, but Fixin' John didn't seem to notice as he passed the metal detector back and forth over one spot. Then, as if snapping out of a trance, Fixin' John came alert again and turned off the metal detector. Taking off the earphones, he motioned for a shovel.

"Let's try digging here," he said. "There's metal

down here, all right, but I don't know if it's big enough to be the gold."

Eagerly Charlie shoveled the sand. This could be it—the moment he had dreamed about. Fixin' John was digging, too, but still there was no sound from Abel Blacklaw. It would be just like him to show up after all the work is done, thought Charlie. A moment later there was a clunk as Charlie's shovel struck a hard object.

"I've got it," he whispered excitedly.

Fixin' John drew a flashlight out of his pocket and trained the beam into the hole. "Go on," he urged. "See if you can bring it up."

Charlie took a deep breath, squared his shoulders, and plunged the shovel into the sand. He struck the object again and worked the shovel down its side until he reached its bottom and then slid it underneath. With a great heave Charlie pushed the handle toward the ground, raising the scoop and its mysterious contents to the surface.

The object was heavy, and the muscles in Charlie's arms twitched from the strain as he raised it high. Then, with a disappointed sigh, he relaxed his grip and let it fall into the hole again. It wasn't pirate's gold. It was just an old tire rim from somebody's car. Angrily Charlie kicked sand into the hole.

"Don't be discouraged, son," said Fixin' John. "That was just our first try. Besides, what happened to all that believing that you're so good at? Remember the power it brings? We'll find the gold for sure if you and I believe."

Charlie thought about how he had felt earlier in

Fixin' John's shop, when he had concentrated on believing. He had felt the power of it then. He had felt it all through his body.

"Yeah. I forgot all about that," he said with a grin. "We'll find it now."

Fixin' John put away his flashlight and handed the metal detector to Charlie. "Here. Let me carry the shovels and you sweep the beach for a while."

Eagerly Charlie took the machine, murmuring an excited thank you as he fitted the earphones over his ears. With the metal detector in his own hands and the power that comes from believing, he was sure to find the gold.

Charlie listened to the soft beeps as they walked along, and he concentrated as hard as he could on believing. Once the beeps speeded up slightly, but when he passed the machine over the spot again, he was sure that whatever had caused the tempo to change was much too small to be a chest of gold. Shrugging, he moved on, aware for the first time that he was on his own beach now.

Waves of tiredness washed over him as he moved on. He had no idea how long he and Fixin' John had been on the beach, but he knew that it was very late, nearly morning, perhaps, because the moon, which had been riding high above Long Island Sound when they began, now seemed to float on the dark water like a golden bubble.

Charlie listened. Had it been his imagination, or had the beeps increased their speed ever so slightly? Beep . . . beep . . . beep. . . . He slowed his steps. They *were* coming faster. He was sure of it now. Beep

. . . beep . . . beep . . . He swept the sand in a wide arc, noting that the beeps slowed again when he pushed the detector to the left. Turning right, he drew in a deep breath and went forward. Beep . . beep . . beep . beep . beepbeepbeep.

Fixin' John must have seen the grin spread across Charlie's face because he dropped the shovels and asked excitedly, "What do you hear, Charlie? Could it be the gold?"

"I think so," said Charlie. "At least it could be!"

"Well, then, let's dig!"

Charlie put aside the metal detector, and the two of them began tossing sand into the air with their shovels. Whatever this was, it was buried deeper than the tire rim had been, and getting it out was going to take some work. Charlie dug with all his might, concentrating on the gold and forgetting for the moment the pouting ghost of Abel Blacklaw and the mysterious intruders who wanted the gold for themselves.

At almost the same moment, his shovel and Fixin' John's struck a solid object beneath the sand.

"It's certainly big enough to be a chest of gold," said Fixin' John. He was puffing and panting from the digging, and he stopped a moment to wipe his forehead with the back of his arm.

Using the shovel like a rake, Charlie scraped the last layer of sand off of the top of the object while Fixin' John brought out his light. Charlie swallowed hard as the beam flashed on, illuminating the lid of an ancient sea chest.

They had found it! They had uncovered pirates' gold!

CHAPTER 19

LOOKING BACK later, Charlie could never be sure of exactly what happened next. He remembered Abel Blacklaw breaking his silence and shouting gleefully that the treasure had been found, but the ghost's words were lost in a barrage of blows on Charlie's back and arms that seemed to come out of nowhere. He reeled and fell to his knees. Beside him, Fixin' John jumped aside and threw his arms up in defense. He was being attacked, too.

"What's happening?" Charlie shouted just before a hard blow landed on his stomach, taking his breath away. "Abel, is that you?" he croaked before his voice had quite returned.

"Of course it's not me. What kind of scoundrel do you think I am? It's *them* is who it is. Captain Finn and Skinhead!"

The words hit Charlie with the same force as the invisible blows of a moment before. *Captain Finn and Skinhead!* It was impossible. But he knew that it was not impossible at all. If Abel Blacklaw could come back as a ghost, then surely Captain Finn and Skinhead could come back as well to claim the gold that he had stolen from them more than two hundred and fifty years before.

Fixin' John jumped into the hole, landing squarely on the lid of the chest, and began swinging the metal detector over his head like a lance. "Keep up your believing," he shouted to Charlie. "We need it *now* more than ever."

Doubt flickered in Charlie's mind for an instant. He didn't have the slightest idea of how to fight an invisible enemy, but believing had worked miracles before. Maybe it would again. He picked up one of the shovels and held it at the ready. The next instant the other shovel raised into the air, too.

"Good work, matey," whispered Abel Blacklaw. "We've got them outnumbered. We'll whip the dogs now."

Suddenly Charlie felt a tug as his feet were pulled out from under him. His shovel went sailing through the air, and he landed on his stomach with a loud *"Oof!"* The salami pressed painfully against his ribs, but before he could twist over onto his side, a heavy weight pressed down on his back. Charlie gasped. He was being sat on by a ghost!

"I've got you now, you thieving devil!" croaked a gravelly voice in his ear. "You'll pay with your life for this."

"Help! Abel! Where are you?" Charlie shouted. His arms were pinned to his sides, but he kicked and flailed with his legs, trying to dislodge his attacker.

Helplessly he watched as Fixin' John was engaged in a battle of his own. The control box and coil dangled by wires from the metal detector, which he was using like a sword as he fenced with a piece of driftwood that lunged and parried through the air seemingly by itself.

"I'll teach ye to steal gold from Captain Finn, you sorry-looking bag of bones. Ye'll be drawn and quartered and hung from the mast." The ghost of Captain Finn let out an enormous laugh and lunged the driftwood harder than ever toward Fixin' John.

Charlie twisted his head sideways and looked up out of the corner of his eye just in time to see something glint in the moonlight. It was a shovel, and it came down with a thud, stopping short just above Charlie's head.

"A little love pat for ye, me darlin' Skinhead," cooed Abel Blacklaw, and the weight that had pressed Charlie to the ground rolled away.

Charlie breathed deeply as the pain from the salami began to subside, but there was no time for coddling himself. The battle was far from over.

Fixin' John was holding his own, but he was panting hard, and Charlie feared that he wouldn't last much longer. Captain Finn must have seen that, too, because he shouted, "Getting tired, are ye, me lily-livered friend? I'll show ye who's the best man here!"

Charlie knew that it was up to him to turn the tide of the fight, but how?

Suddenly he thought of a way, and he took off at a run, shouting over his shoulder as he went. "I'll be back in a minute with reinforcements!"

The answer was simple. The salami. Abel Blacklaw had wanted it as a distraction, but he would use it as an *attraction* instead.

He raced across the two private beaches and then slowed and crept silently up to the house where Rasputin and the man in baggy undershorts lived. There was an open window near the back door, and Charlie crouched beneath it and drew the salami out of his shirt. Nearly gagging, he unwrapped it and held it up to the window. Rasputin would be sure to smell it no matter how far away from the window he slept. Charlie held his nose and breathed through his mouth, but even then the nauseous odor got through.

Come on, Rasputin, he begged silently. I can't hold on much longer.

Charlie crouched there, listening, for what was becoming an almost unbearable length of time. His arm was going numb from holding the salami over his head, and the terrible smell was making his stomach roll. Then, just as he was about to give up and slink away in defeat, he heard what sounded like the whine of a dog. Charlie cocked his ear and listened with all his might. There it was again, and this time he was sure that it was Rasputin.

He slipped behind a bush and waited, his heart beating in anticipation. A moment later the back door opened and Rasputin nosed out, followed by the man in baggy undershorts.

"Hurry up and do your job," he said in a voice thick with sleep. "Pugh! Don't roll in whatever's making that *awful* smell."

With that he hurried back into the house, closing the door behind him. Charlie waved the salami through the branches of the bush, and Rasputin trotted down the steps and hurried toward it.

"Hello, fella," said Charlie, giving him a friendly pat, and the dog returned the greeting with a wag. "Come on with me. I've got something for you to do."

Holding the reeking salami just out of Rasputin's

reach, Charlie galloped off toward the battle, with the dog loping along behind. As they drew near, Charlie was relieved to see that Fixin' John was still on his feet and engaged in his fencing match with Captain Finn. The sound of grunts and curses were coming from a spot beyond the hole which held the chest, and Charlie knew that Abel and Skinhead were locked in heavy combat.

Charlie put a hand on Rasputin, hesitating for an instant to lead him on. Abel had said that dogs have a special sense when it comes to ghosts, and he was counting on that to end the fight.

As they inched forward, Rasputin seemed to forget about the salami, and a low rumble started in his throat. He lowered his sleek black body and began to slink toward his invisible prey. The growl grew louder, and as it did, the driftwood sword quivered in the air for an instant and then dropped to the ground with a *smack*. Somewhere beyond the open hole Skinhead was silent, but Abel Blacklaw let out a howl.

"Have ye gone mad, matey? You've unleashed the monster dog!"

Fixin' John was at Charlie's side now, with perspiration flowing down his face and a wide grin on his face.

"You saved me, boy. I couldn't have held on much longer."

"Now we've got to save Abel," said Charlie. "He's terrified of Rasputin."

The big dog broke into a run, snarling and sniffing the ground as he circled the treasure chest. Sand was flying everywhere as Rasputin went after his prey.

"Abel!" shouted Charlie. "Come here quickly and get between Fixin' John and me. We'll protect you."

"But how?" came the whimpering reply.

"You've just got to *believe!*"

Almost before he got the words out, Charlie felt an invisible hand on his arm. "It'll be okay," he whispered to Abel. "You'll see."

"Let's get out of here!" shrieked Captain Finn, and there was a loud splash, followed by another. Rasputin made a beeline for the water but stopped at the edge and paced back and forth, growling out toward the sea.

"Whew! They're gone," said Fixin' John. "I hope it's for good."

"Aye. They'll not be back. They're as cowardly a pair as ever there was," said Abel, but Charlie could feel that the ghost had not moved so much as one inch from his side.

Suddenly Rasputin stopped his pacing and perked up his ears. The others listened, too, as off in the distance the man in baggy undershorts was calling Rasputin home.

"Go on, boy. Go on home," urged Charlie. He felt a twinge of regret that he had tricked Rasputin and promised himself to reward the dog soon. Rasputin turned and trotted off in the direction of home, leaving Charlie and Fixin' John and the ghost of Abel Blacklaw alone once more with the chest of gold.

CHAPTER 20

"WE'LL NEVER be able to haul it up," Abel Black-law cautioned. "It's far too heavy for that."

"Then what do you suggest we do?" asked Fixin' John.

"Well, the way I see it," said the ghost importantly, "we'd better make the hole wider and open up the chest down there. That way we can bring up the gold a few sacks at a time."

Charlie and Fixin' John both nodded their agreement and each picked up a shovel and began to dig.

"Since there are only two shovels, I'll be more than glad to hold the torch," offered Abel in a syrupy voice.

Exchanging a knowing glance with Charlie, Fixin' John fished in his pocket and drew out the flashlight, which Abel Blacklaw took from his hand.

The light hung suspended like a small moon in the dark sky, and under its beam the old metal sea chest glinted dully.

Charlie's shoulders ached and beside him Fixin' John puffed and panted as he lifted the shovelfuls of sand, but they dug down deeper and deeper until the latch was exposed and a trench had been cut along all four sides of the chest so that the lid could be opened with ease.

Finally the moment arrived. The hole was wide enough and deep enough to open the chest of gold.

"I think you should be the one to open it, Abel, since you're the one who put it here," said Charlie.

"I agree," said Fixin' John.

"It would be a pleasure," replied the ghost with obvious pride.

Charlie took the flashlight from Abel's invisible hand and trained the beam on the latch. For the next few seconds grunts and gasps filled the air, but the lid did not budge.

"It's just a mite stuck," grumbled the ghost as a shovel rose into the air and cracked down, shattering the ancient metal of the latch. "There. That should do it. We'll for sure get her open now."

Charlie crossed his fingers and held his breath. On the other side of the hole, Fixin' John looked nervous, too. Then, with a loud squeak of protest the lid, which had been closed for more than two hundred and fifty years, began slowly to rise. Charlie crouched forward, nearly losing his balance, as he tried to see into the chest.

"Auk! I've been robbed!" The cry came from Abel Blacklaw as the lid flung back, revealing an empty chest. "Some thieving devil has stolen my gold!"

It was too awful to be true. After all their work, the gold was gone. Charlie sank back in the sand unable to speak. Fixin' John shook his head over and over again and stared into the chest, which held only a thin film of sand, and Abel Blacklaw began to sob and mutter sorrowfully to himself.

At first Charlie paid no attention to the words that the ghost was mumbling. He had miserable-enough thoughts of his own. But suddenly he snapped to attention and listened, unable to believe what he heard.

"Oh, Nanabelle. Poor Nanabelle. All's lost now."

"Nanabelle!" shrieked Charlie. "What does Nanabelle have to do with this?"

The ghost heaved a great sigh and then, in a apologetic voice, he said, "Aye, matey, I've a confession to make. The gold was never for you. 'Twas for your darlin' sister, Nanabelle, whom I've loved with all me heart since first I set eyes on her."

"Oh, don'tcha fear, matey. I would have given ye a sack or two for helping to dig it up, and a sack for Fixin' John, too, for without ye, I could never have done it. But the rest was for Nanabelle, the only true love of me heart."

Charlie stood up, stretching himself to his full height and rammed his fists into his pockets.

"Do you mean to say that you got me to dig up a chest of gold just so that you could give it to *her?*" he cried, still unable to believe the ghost's words. "Then why did you play all those rotten tricks on her, like dropping an egg on her head and tying her hair to a chair? Answer me *that!*"

"I couldn't have ye suspecting me real motives, now could I, matey?" said Abel in a cunning voice. "Besides, have ye noticed the spark of fire in her eyes when she's riled?"

"I've noticed it," grumbled Charlie. "A few more times than I've wanted to, thanks to you."

Fixin' John gathered up the remnants of his metal

detector and smiled sympathetically at Charlie. "I'm sorry that it turned out this way, son."

Charlie shrugged. "I guess we might as well go home," he mumbled. Beaming the light into the chest, he sighed and took one last look. As he stared sadly at the dusting of sand in the bottom, he gradually became aware of scratches on the floor of the chest. What had seemed at first to be only random scratches now suddenly appeared to have a pattern.

"Hey. Let's pull up the chest," he shouted. "I think there's a message carved into the bottom."

With a burst of new energy Charlie began tugging at one end of the chest. Fixin' John pulled on the other, and together they lifted the empty box out of the hole and onto the beach. Charlie brushed aside the sand with his hand and trained the beam of the flashlight on the message.

TO ABEL BLACKLAW

WHEN YOU AND CAPTAIN FINN AND SKINHEAD
FAILED TO COME BACK I SWAM ASHORE AND
FINDING YOUR MOUND OF FRESHLY DUG DIRT I
OPENED HER UP AND MOVED THE GOLD TO A
SPOT OF ME OWN.
IF YE BE ALIVE AND COME BACK LOOKING FOR
IT I THOUGHT YOU'D LIKE TO KNOW.

BAITFISH

"*Rotten, thieving cutthroat!*" screeched the ghost. "What does he mean by stealing *my* gold!"

It was well past noon when Charlie awoke the

next day, and he could barely remember stumbling home and falling into bed with all his clothes on. He had no memory whatever of bringing home the shovels, and he made a mental note to check the garage if he ever decided to get up. What he did remember was the empty chest and how he and Fixin' John had put it back into the hole and buried it again while Abel Blacklaw slunk off somewhere to pout.

Charlie sat up in bed and stretched his arms up over his head, yawning deeply. He couldn't remember ever being so tired, and he started to go back under his covers when an odd feeling came over him. Glancing quickly around the room and finding nothing particularly unusual, he scanned more slowly, noting each object as his eyes swept past. The door was closed and firmly latched. An empty root-beer can sat on the sill of the window where sunlight streamed in. There was the usual jumble of papers and candy wrappers on his desk. Nothing unusual about that, he thought and shifted his gaze to the fireplace.

There he stopped and sat stiffly erect. It was gone. The gravestone that only he had been able to see was gone. "It's me calling card," the ghost had said, and Charlie knew that with its disappearance, the ghost of Abel Blacklaw was gone, too.

A lump formed in Charlie's throat. For all of Abel's mischief and conniving, for all his grumpiness and tricks on Nanabelle that had gotten Charlie into trouble several times, he knew that he was really going to miss the ghost. I didn't matter that he would never be rich. It only mattered that Abel Blacklaw was gone, and the beach would never be the same.

Charlie dragged himself slowly out of bed and

went to the window, gazing at the sea gulls that flocked across the sand and wondering sadly if Abel Blacklaw was among them.

Suddenly thoughts began to churn in Charlie's mind, and a big grin spread across his face. Baitfish had said that he had moved the gold to a spot of his own. If that was true, it could still be somewhere on the beach. Not only that, but Henry was coming down from Poughkeepsie this very night. Henry would believe. He knew that he would. Then with Henry believing and Charlie believing and Fixin' John believing, surely they could get the metal detector working again and find the gold. And if they did, Abel Blacklaw just might come back.

Charlie wasn't sleepy anymore. What was more, he wasn't even the least bit tired, and he hurried to his desk and began to draw a treasure map.